Loose Ends
by
Adam Parish

Book 3 of the
Jack Edwards and Amanda Barratt mystery series

Also by Adam Parish
The Quartermaster (1)
Parthian Shot (2)

To sign up for offers, updates
and find out more about Adam Parish
visit our website www.adam-parish.com

Text copyright @2021 by Adam Parish

ISBN 979-8-5988-7260-4

Thanks to Helen
for her help,
humour,
and patience.

Chapter 1

As reunions went, this one promised to be poor. There were just two guests, only one of whom was invited. The other was going to end up dead.

Bobby Lennon shut his car door with care. Satisfied that it was invisible from the distant road, he pushed the Browning pistol down the back of his jeans and made his way into the tightly bunched canopy of conifers. Dawn had just broken, but little light penetrated the copse, and the irregular ground forced Lennon to be careful with his footing. After a short, deliberate passage, he halted behind a large pine and viewed the extensive, sparse upland moorland beyond. A quarter of a mile distant, a small, still, black lochan broke the ground, and on the far side stood a rude wooden hut. Beyond, the uneven peat-patched ground inclined to the horizon, and below this lay cliffs which descended precipitously to the sea.

Lennon was a tall, powerful man of about forty and he was armed. He had surprise on his side and he had experience. His heart thumped. It wasn't easy to kill a man, especially a man as unpredictable as Brannigan, rogue voices in his head screamed.

He hadn't seen Brannigan for a year or so, but he had known him and worked with him for many years. Theoretically, Lennon was the better man with his infantry and special forces background. Brannigan, while generally acknowledged as smarter, had never exhibited an interest in violence. He was tall and spare and was nicknamed "the Hippie". Why he had been a member of the special forces had always been a mystery to Lennon. It had always been assumed that Lennon would prevail in a physical contest, but as he considered this, he had enough sense to acknowledge that he had never seen him tested or even scared. Brannigan demanded respect.

Brannigan was certainly unconventional, and although he owned a permanent dwelling in nearby Kinlochkerran, a village ten or so miles to the north, he was rarely to be found there. More usually, he could be located on the land that he owned near Southness, a barren, generally unusable acreage at the end of the peninsula. The shed adjacent to the lochan was the only building that Lennon knew of on the plot, but in the high summer Brannigan could be anywhere.

Lennon waited. Long, drawn-out, tense minutes passed without any change in the vista before a drop of water splashing onto his nose from an overhanging pine tree made up his mind. He removed his Browning, readied it and then broke cover, moving warily towards the hut.

It took thirty seconds, but it felt longer before he stood before the unprepossessing wooden door. The hut was windowless so he deferred a frontal assault, instead diving to the ground at the rear of the building and pressing his ear to the shabby timbers. The only sound he could hear was his thumping heart, but that soon disappeared into background noise, and after a few seconds' intense listening he received nothing from within. Pistol in hand, he returned to the front door and slowly persuaded it open. He moved inside.

The hut was cluttered, but not untidy nor unclean. A sniff of a single discarded tin of tuna and the sell-by dates of a couple of similar tins in a plastic bag hanging by a nail told Lennon that it had been occupied recently. Against the far wall and along its width lay a mattress with well-ordered bedding. There was shelving above, home to a variety of tinned foodstuffs and a kettle with tea and coffee. A variety of practical tools were scattered around the hut: fishing rods, a spade and, as Lennon looked more closely, a shotgun. He wondered whether he had use for this but decided to stay on plan.

He considered his next move. It was true that an unknown length of wait within the hut might allow him decisive surprise, but a confined space such as this was likely to offer up forensic and trace evidence. Given Lennon's other advantages, he could take his chances outdoors. With luck, he could quarter the high ground and take Brannigan there, leaving his death looking accidental. Maybe he could entice him near the precipitous cliffs to the south.

His mind made up, Lennon opened the creaking door. As he did so, he instantly regretted not giving more weight to a low but audible noise his brain had registered, but not analysed, a second earlier. The lochan sat, still, black and disinterested, ahead of him. More urgent was the crude and irregular length of pinewood that moved towards him and then struck him furiously across the face. A curtain of blood obscured his sight. Lennon was tough; the blow didn't knock him out, but it knocked him down and he fell heavily on his back onto rocky ground. The shooting pain was mostly from his left eye, but he was conscious. He squinted through his good eye and saw exactly what he had expected and feared.

Brannigan stood over him, very close. He was roughly dressed and his beard and unkempt hair gave him a wild look. A further discouraging glance confirmed him as fit and vital. Brannigan was a man of very few words and, as he took a half stride forward, Lennon knew he was now very close to death. He tried to reach round for the Browning, but his body did not respond. Something that might have been a smile seemed to pass over the features of Brannigan as he drew back the log for a further and perhaps final strike. However, in a contest that had already contained a few surprises, Lennon's groping fingers had clasped a knife that he kept strapped to his thigh, and in a single desperate movement he threw it in Brannigan's general direction.

There was a lot of luck in life, and so it proved in death as the knife, out of a million possible outcomes, lodged deeply and beautifully in Brannigan's neck. The vague smile never left his face. For a moment nothing happened, and then a high-pressure spray of warm, red blood exploded. Brannigan kept smiling. Then he fell dead.

Lennon gasped for breath and wiped his face with his forearm. He rolled a yard from the lifeless body and took stock of the various pains in his own aching body. He drew his hand across his face again. It was covered in blood. Some of it was his own blood, but further wiping and stroking of his face reassured him that any major loss had been largely staunched. He opened and shut both eyes a few times. Both were working. He urged himself on and prepared to stand. This proved unexpectedly easy, and Lennon was ready to consider the problem of the body. Although they had been close in the death struggle, he was relieved that there had been no direct physical contact. That was about all the good news. The bad news included removal of the knife stuck deep in Brannigan's neck, the fact that Lennon's clothes were covered in blood, and the extent of his unknown injuries. All of these challenges could be overcome, but what was going to be difficult was Brannigan's six-foot frame lying out in the open.

Whatever Lennon's plan had been, this was not it. His head was clearing and he looked around. As expected, there was no one there, although so much had gone wrong so far anything was possible. He reviewed the position and confirmed his priorities: remove the knife, get rid of his clothing, and hide the body. This last task could only be achieved on a temporary basis. He wasn't happy with the hut as a temporary mortuary; it would provide concealment but risk him leaving trace evidence. Indeed, moving the body at all was a big risk. But so was indecision, so Lennon went back into the hut. A black plastic bag would just about do it. He tore two off the roll and wrapped them firmly around his hands and arms.

He grabbed the cold hands and dragged Brannigan into the hut. It wasn't that easy a job, pulling the body and avoiding contact in the small area, but he was strong and his balance didn't let him down. Once he had the full length of the body into the hut, he tip-toed around the cadaver and out. He shut the hut door. He was now perspiring feverishly. The sun was hardly warm but it seemed to pierce his skull, and his temples throbbed uncontrollably. His brain was now working, however, and he moved rapidly back to the copse. Lennon had come to kill and he was prepared. He selected a depression created by an upturned tree. It was deep and the sub-soil was soft. From his car, he produced a spade and dug down about two or three feet. He stripped and buried his clothes, including socks and shoes. He had spare clothes and quickly fashioned himself a new outfit from the eclectic garments.

This done, he returned to his car. He lit a cigarette and reviewed the position. He had left no trace evidence and none of his blood was on Brannigan. With luck, the body would lie undiscovered for a while. He looked into the car mirror and inspected his face, wiping away some remaining spots of blood. It was good news – there wasn't going to be a major scar nor an injury that he couldn't explain away.

Most of his plan had gone wrong, but it wasn't a disaster. He was alive and Brannigan was dead, and that was a start.

Chapter 2

A second cigarette calmed his shaking hands and Lennon threw the butt out of the car window. He glanced at his watch. It was eight – about ten minutes since he had killed Brannigan and about five since he had hauled his body into the hut. Despite the remote nature of the location, that was too long at the scene. He started the car.

Lennon stayed lucky. The road was deserted. He was about five miles north of town and drove conservatively until he emerged in its outskirts, satisfied that he had not been observed anywhere near the scene.

A ten-minute drive took him through Longtown and to the tiny village of Canish and his large villa. His unfired gun would be better returned. At this hour, Val wouldn't be up. These days if she beat noon it was an accomplishment.

He settled on the back door and through the kitchen, past an empty vodka bottle and a tumbler half full, and then to his study. He didn't study anything, but the house was large for just two of them. He replaced the gun in his drawer and retraced his steps. His mobile rang and he looked at the number. It had to be answered, but he managed to make the call short.

He reviewed the rest of his day. He was running a little late for his meeting with his business partner. That was going to be fun. Adam Jardine was a weasel, although Lennon imagined Jardine had some choice words to describe him too. Lennon had financed the business and Jardine did the work. But Jardine had got too big for his boots. Had he really believed Lennon was just going to roll over and hand over a larger share out of the goodness of his heart? For once, the law and the partnership arrangement had been on Lennon's side, so they had gone on.

Jardine had been a good choice of partner a decade or so back. He was local and had connections through his brother to a larger company who, in this part of the world, were generally able to guarantee endless sub-contract work. It was a miracle they'd been so successful, really, given how much they hated each other. Jardine had tried to keep it all legal at first, offering numerous times to buy out Lennon's controlling share, but he'd always refused. At first because the price offered was too low, but eventually for no reason other than it pissed Jardine off. And that was the best reason going.

But Jardine had begun to secure the share of profits that he apparently so richly deserved through tendering low official prices – often to his brothers' company – and collecting the remainder separately. It had taken Lennon quite a while to uncover the nature of the fraud. He would be first to admit he was neither trained nor indeed interested in business. He had long since, and many times over, recovered his investment, but if he could just get Jardine on the back foot, it would be the right leverage to secure a huge walk-away offer.

Adam Jardine wasn't that smart and he wasn't that scary. Lennon could handle him. Adam would get the money from his brothers and that would be that. Lennon allowed himself a brief thought about Adam's brother. Eddie Jardine would be well over fifty now and he was tougher than his younger brother. Still, he was wealthy, had kids and was respectable now. He would have no trouble there.

He carelessly swung his car into the headquarters car park and decided he would keep Jardine waiting for another few minutes. He mulled over his only other appointment today. He was less clear on the reasons for this appointment, but was far more enthusiastic about keeping it. He had wanted her for years, and, he mused pleasurably, it seemed that he was, at last, getting somewhere. It had been frustrating that she had denied him for years, but Lennon could put up with pleasure deferred if the deferment lasted only until today.

He locked and left the car and completed the short walk. Jardine had certainly done a good job. The scruffy yard and wooden hut of a decade ago had been triumphantly overlaid with a modern office building and a tarred yard with multiple modern workshops. He ignored the screams from the meaningless health and safety notices as he walked through the already nearly full car park and into the office building.

Lennon vaguely nodded at the receptionist, ignoring her offers of assistance, and made his way to Jardine's office. A light knock on the door did not delay his progress. Jardine was behind his desk, poring over a large set of plans. He did not look up. Lennon didn't wait for an acknowledgement and made his way to an empty desk alongside.

The desk had been there for years and had been installed when, in a brief period of rapprochement, Lennon had agreed to actually do some work for the business. It had, to date, never been used in anger, at least by him. He flopped easily into the fake leather chair and stretched his legs onto the top of the desk. He looked across at Jardine, but said nothing. Why should he? He held all the cards.

Jardine continued to pore over the plans, but Lennon could sense that he had lost concentration. As if to confirm his thinking, Jardine broke the silence and came straight to the point.

"I've got all the papers drawn up and the money in place. So, we're good to go."

He paused at that point and looked hard at Lennon with what Lennon imagined was his game face. Lennon wondered how long

Jardine could keep it up. Not long, Lennon wagered, and he won the bet within a few seconds.

"Well?"

Lennon smiled at him malignantly and muttered, "I'm thinking about it."

It was too much for Jardine this time. "Fuck sake, Bobby. Thinking about what? You've had ten years to think about it."

It was a pretty fair question – well aimed for, in truth, Lennon wasn't thinking about anything remotely related to the sale of his shares. Five hundred thousand pounds for an investment of fifty thousand represented a very good outcome. Maybe he could get more?

He considered a moment. It wasn't that he was greedy for money. It was about the only vice he didn't have. It was just that he hated Jardine. They had been friends once, but that had been twenty years ago. He wondered why he hated Jardine and could not come up with a single reason. They had been inseparable for years. "Bobby and Adam," everybody had called them. The likeliest of likely lads. And then they had just gradually drifted apart. Lennon wasn't a native of these parts and Jardine was. He had family and extended family in the area; folks that had been here for centuries. Lennon had no one. He had had a mother for the first twelve years of his life, but she had died and left him alone. Then in and out of inner-city Glasgow orphanages. The staff had meant well, but it had all been duty and not love. He had survived sustained by one dream, and it came true when he was accepted into the army on his sixteenth birthday.

Jardine was waiting for an answer.

Lennon said blandly, "I was wondering about it. I was talking to Val. She said that it might be worth more and maybe I should get a professional valuation."

Jardine sighed. A nerve twitched in his neck. "Come on, Bobby. You know that this is way over the odds. Look, if you don't take this now, I might take it off the table." He drummed his fingers on the table.

Lennon let a slow smirk spread across his face. "I enjoy watching a man raising with a lousy hand."

Jardine's face fell and he broke eye contact. Lennon rose and walked across to stand opposite him. Very near. He paused, forcing Jardine to lift his head. "Well, Adam. You do what you need to do. I think I'll mull this over a little more."

And with that, Lennon turned and, without a backward glance, left the office, laughing as he went. He could feel Jardine's eyes boring into his back and he made sure to take his time and revel in it.

Chapter 3

Two hundred miles further north on the west coast of Scotland, Jack Edwards stared out of his bay window. The window needed a clean but that didn't matter. Outside, the scene was impressive. Wandering seabirds, irregular and dramatic cliffs, an endless blue ocean and an even more impressive blue sky. It was a view he had enjoyed many times and he never tired of it, but today it could command neither his interest nor his enthusiasm, and he turned away from the window and fell into a deep, winged armchair. He lightly shut his eyes and enjoyed the sun's warmth on his face.

It had been nearly four years since he had lost her, but when he really tried, the image he conjured up in his mind was still vivid, although very slowly fading. He tried every day to halt the dwindling of his memory but he knew it was a losing battle. He opened his eyes and glanced at the only photograph he had of her. The summit she stood on rose from behind the house, gently past the quarry and up precipitous slopes to a rocky summit. It was an exhilarating walk and an unrivalled viewpoint, and Jack loved walking hills. He had kept the quarry open to preserve the local jobs – it's what she wanted – but he never went up that hill.

He returned to the photograph. Her bobbish, thick red locks and piercing green eyes looked straight at him. She was smiling, not for the camera but at him. He smiled back, and with his visual memory refreshed, he shut his eyes again. At first, he was comfortable, but it got tougher as he speculated about how their life together would have worked out. These thoughts became unbearable when he reflected on her pregnancy. Medical and political opinion varied about the term length that made a child, but to Jack it would have been a child – *his* child. This was too uncomfortable; he needed her help.

How can I carry on? he asked. *Move on*, came the reply. *Don't be sad forever. Don't think about us every day.* He protested that he wasn't ready to take that advice yet, and she told him not to be silly. His thoughts darkened again, as they always did. Four years on he could, mostly, defend himself against the voices in his head that screamed that their deaths were his fault, but the guilt could only ever be partially mitigated. He had brought her here, and he hadn't kept her safe. He would never get past that.

As to moving on, whatever that meant, if it meant romance in any form, that was going to be tough. He had had a problem with commitment all his adult life. Falling in love meant giving yourself to another person, and if you did that you were certain to get hurt. He had never really found anyone with whom he was prepared to make this trade. Until Marion, of course. And he had lost her.

He opened his eyes. These were unhealthy thoughts. Maybe he *should* move on. At just under forty he wasn't completely past it. He had a lot of money and was reasonable-looking. There were a few other things to his credit that even an impartial observer might allow, but all that taken together still wasn't really convincing.

There was another problem – he didn't know any suitable partners, except perhaps for Amanda. Marion and Amanda had been friends and Marion would have surely approved. They were superficially unalike: Marion a softly spoken academic, Amanda operating in a more dangerous arena. But underneath they were similar – strong and entirely comfortable with the world and their place in it. Jack envied that.

He liked Amanda, and he thought that she liked him. Surprisingly, he also had enjoyed some of the times when she had involved him in her work. This worried him a bit. He mostly agreed with her about which side to take, but her world was full of shades of grey with a host of morally relative choices. Worse, these fine decisions had to be taken often on instinct and usually very quickly. And then some people ended up dead. He decided not to focus upon the ones that he had killed, and he jumped out of his seat with resolution and walked across to the window. He had another free day, like every day, and he wondered what to do.

His phone interrupted.

An enthusiastic voice said, "Hello, Jack." Clive Beck was his accountant, and he loved being an accountant. He gushed on. "Glad I caught you."

Jack wasn't. "Oh, hello, Clive."

Beck got straight to business. "I was hoping I would have caught up with you last week. You said you would be in town."

This was true. Jack didn't have any excuse, so he didn't bother making one up.

"Anyway, Smith's been telephoning me – every day. We need to tell him something."

Smith was a young local entrepreneur who had submitted a proposal for the development of some kind of specialist drilling bits. Jack hadn't read the proposal.

Beck went on, "Well, what do you think? Twenty thousand pounds. His projections look good, and I like the look of him."

Jack had met Smith once and he seemed a decent prospect. "What do you think, Clive?"

"I'm for it."

"Okay, go ahead. I'll catch up with you soon." Jack was hopeful that this decisiveness would end the conversation, but it didn't.

Beck cleared his throat and said cautiously, "I wanted to talk to you about the hotel renovation project."

Jack groaned inwardly. In a wild act about a year ago, possibly in response to his ongoing despair, he had purchased a derelict hotel hundreds of miles from his home and initiated an ambitious project of restoration. For most of his adult life, he had been employed as a fairly unprepossessing lecturer at an unfashionable university. His fiscal management had been weak. But that had changed when his aunt's money had come his way. It had made him careful, even mean. Having escaped the financial anxieties of the herd, he was absolutely determined never to re-join them.

Was he happier? At least that question was an easy one. Money *did* make you happier, and that was just that. It gave you access to pretty much anything you wanted and it saved you time. Whether he was actually happy was an entirely different question, but whatever the answer, he was never giving the money back.

Beck continued gently. "Moore's been on the phone. He seemed pretty happy, but you know architects."

Jack did. They would spend any given amount of money.

"All his reports seem in order, but really we could do with a visit. Check up on progress, that sort of thing. Moore's not very experienced."

Jack laughed. "Look, I know you were never in favour of the project."

"True enough, but you're the boss. It's your two million pounds. Still, we need to catch up with him. He says everything's on target but we should go there and see for ourselves."

Beck was quite right. There was no category on a balance sheet for impulse purchases aimed at mending a broken heart.

"I know a good man locally," Beck said. "Lot of experience with this sort of thing. He's semi-retired. I can send him down and commission a report?"

Jack stubbed out his cigarette and rose. This was his folly and maybe he should take some responsibility. "Let me think about this. I'll give you a ring back today."

He looked at the armchair but decided not to return to it and drifted from the room and outside to think. That took a minute or so, for his baronial-style mansion, which occupied a solitary situation near the edge of the highest point round the bay, was large.

He lived alone, but he liked that the house size meant he could have any number of guests or friends around at any time. The fact he never did didn't matter.

He ambled from his front door onto a short well-defined path that curled up to the edge of the unguarded cliffs, and sat on a large wooden bench. He lit another cigarette and, scanning the recently opened packet, calculated that this was his eighth of the morning. That was too many, and although he felt pretty good, he promised himself a period of restraint to begin at an unspecified future time.

His mind settled on the hotel project. He was not as excited as he should be for a man who had just spent around two million pounds. The Lake Hotel had a long-held fascination for him. Situated on the south-west coast of Scotland, with views to Northern Ireland and the Ayrshire coast, the hotel enjoyed an enviable setting. It was three storeys high, a brilliantly painted white oblong. An art deco, perhaps late brutalist school, the surreal design of an eccentric naval commander in the early part of the twentieth century. As a building, it was impressive, for those that liked that sort of thing. Jack did. It was the sort of building that would have been normal in Kensington High Street but quite unique at the end of a bleak and remote Scottish peninsula.

This combination had enchanted him some twelve months ago, but now he was not so sure. The history of the hotel – it had been commandeered by the military in World War Two – and then the desperately romantic stories of the subsequent owners who heroically tried to make an enduring business had all appealed to him. On a whim, realising that he could easily finance such a folly, he had surprised himself by going ahead with the project. Whether the loss of Marion had inspired this uncharacteristic move hardly mattered now. What did matter was what he was going to do with the restored building.

He had no business plan, nor indeed any plan whatsoever. He also knew that, whatever happened, he would never prefer it to his home in Mascar. He lit a ninth cigarette and, with a burst of determination, got up, returned to the house and prepared to leave.

Chapter 4

The roads were dry and the Maserati roared south effortlessly. It was mid-afternoon now and only an occasional vehicle had checked his stately progress. He was about halfway there with about ninety miles to cover.

He came upon a small town and considered a stop. Tiredness killed, they said, but Jack wasn't tired and decided instead to childishly play with the car's throttle, the resultant roar alarming a small group of tourists on what must have been a high street. After a further couple of unnecessary gear changes, he left the metropolis behind and back to the deserted and narrow A-roads.

He was in high spirits, singing along tunelessly to relentless rock music, and he gained many miles before pulling over at an interesting sea-hugging viewpoint. He was on the west side of the peninsula now and there were islands out to sea. The nearest was impressively mountainous. He wasn't sure whether it had been formed by erupting volcanoes or what – his geology was weak. Whatever, they had been there a long time.

As he lit a cigarette, Jack observed with dissatisfaction that the skin on his hand was looking a little leathery, even aged. His hands were less than four decades old, but probably further through their life cycle than the stately island heights. The mountains would ultimately be swept into the sea, but they would outlive the flesh on his hands. It wasn't a great thought on a beautiful day, so he dismissed it. He drew on the cigarette, looked out of the car window out to sea and started up the car. He had a good run down the east coast of the peninsula and soon arrived at the unprepossessing county town of Longtown.

It was a strange part of the world. Although connected to the mainland, it was more of an island, and it had all the virtues and vices of any isolated outpost. It was home to a few thousand folks, far fewer than in its heyday as a centre of whisky production. But that trade, like everything else, had been taken over by faceless multinational companies and the town struggled on, powerless to check the relentless slow depletion of its population. There wasn't much fishing nowadays either, despite a surprisingly modern and extensive harbour, and the town eked out a living by providing services to a declining agricultural sector.

Jack wondered what would become of the area in a hundred years' time. He wasn't confident. None of this mattered today, though. He wasn't going to live for a hundred years, and he hadn't bought the derelict hotel as a business venture. It was an indulgence and he could afford it. At least the gentle decline of the area kept the masses away and allowed him to enjoy it in peace and quiet. Especially the world-class golf course, which was nearly always empty.

The hotel was sited some ten miles south of Longtown on the southernmost part of the peninsula. Despite progress, it was not yet habitable, so Jack had rented one of a set of large, bleached sandstone villas which sat opposite the golf course. It was expensive, but it was comfortable and superbly convenient. He should have just bought one of these villas rather than indulging himself with the money pit, but where was the fun in that?

It took about a minute and a half to clear Longtown from north to south, and the final leg of the journey consisted of a four-mile westerly drive to the villa through scruffy-looking agricultural land until a very small sign announced the village of Canish. It consisted of a few sandstone villas, a small collection of council houses and a large and high-class hotel. This hotel had been popular once, but had closed and reinvented itself as luxury digs for golfers. The golf course at Canish was on every serious golfer's bucket list and, luckily for the hotel, golfers were older and wealthier than most tourists and came from all over the world.

Jack's rented villa was the third of a group of six, built originally by Victorian businessmen but nowadays usually let for tourist golfers. Each villa could comfortably house about half a dozen.

He pulled into the extensive gravelled driveway through an ungated entrance and carelessly parked the car. He got out, stretched a bit and ambled back towards the road, across which sat the rolling sandy fairways of the golf course. It was lightly peopled as ever, despite it being the summer and the weather reasonable, albeit with the ever-present powerful wind.

He leant on the wall for a moment and took in the view of the course with the sea beyond. That's why folks had to play it at least once. As he did so, a car passed him, slowed, and turned into the adjacent villa. Jack turned his head cautiously and watched a man and woman alighting and beginning to extract shopping. He decided to introduce himself, and he crossed the lawned area and leant over the dividing wall.

The man was in the house with the first shopping run. The woman looked across to Jack.

He broke the ice. "Hello."

She nodded and, flashing him a smile, laid down a couple of bags and moved towards him.

"I'm Jack Edwards. I'm your new neighbour." He held out his hand and she took it.

"Suzie Miller."

"Holiday?"

She shook her head. "No, we live here," she said in a pleasant local accent. "You?"

"I've taken it for three months. Bit of golf and a little work."

She nodded and he conducted a quick review of his neighbour. Suzie Miller was about forty-five and quite an attractive woman. She was tall and slim, had short, bushy black hair and attractive and alert blue eyes. She would be okay as a neighbour.

However, where there was an attractive woman, there was often a man, and he emerged from a side door of the house and joined them.

"This is my husband, Peter. Peter, this is Jack Edwards. He's going to be our neighbour for the next three months."

Peter Miller's face received this news unenthusiastically, but he extended his hand. "Nice to meet you, Jack."

"Jack is going to do a bit of golfing," his wife said.

Routinely, and in a tone that suggested he had no intention of doing so, Peter Miller suggested that they might have a game together, and Jack tentatively agreed.

He was older than Jack, and quite a bit older than his wife. His accent had a bit of local in it, but was blended with some received pronunciation that made him easy to place as not local but difficult to deduce further. He was tall, well preserved, and still had most of his hair. He looked at Jack and, without smiling, ostentatiously put his arm round his wife's waist. Then he held her hand.

The conversation seemed over and Jack said, "I'll let you get on with unpacking. I hope we can see something of each other."

He hadn't meant to, but he directed this remark more at Suzie than her husband and, innocent as this exit line had been, he could tell Peter Miller had noted and resented it.

Chapter 5

Amanda Barratt emerged from the depths of Russell Square Tube Station and enjoyed the fresh air, if not the heavy rain, of the Bloomsbury morning. It wasn't the most popular terminus for daily London commuters, and the exiting passengers quickly dispersed and fused easily into the morning rush. Amanda now had a walk of about a quarter of a mile or so, although she wasn't entirely sure because today was the first day of her new job.

Amanda glanced down at her outfit. Orthodox, but expensive. She looked like any other high-powered female city executive, she supposed. Except she was that and more. She had been a publisher and a policewoman, eventually achieving a commandership in the Metropolitan Police. Next, a high-level role in MI5. Now, at last, at the age of thirty-eight, her own department.

It wasn't a big department. To the public there was only MI5 and MI6. However, around the time of World War One, some ten MI (military intelligence) departments had been created. This rose to seventeen by the end of World War Two. Gradually, these individual departments had been wound up or absorbed. As far as the public were concerned, there were only two left.

Both of the remaining branches were now subject to unprecedented public scrutiny. But the activities of secret security services sat awkwardly in a democratic spotlight. And some had no place there at all.

MI1 had been set up in World War One and had been responsible for such diverse activities as interception, wireless telegraphy, cryptanalysis and the general distribution of intelligence. Its various sub-departments had been absorbed and merged, eventually morphing into GCHQ. Government Communications Headquarters was top secret, so naturally everyone knew they were based in Cheltenham and employed many thousands. Open government required that their chief executive and senior management were public figures, and parliamentary committees enquired and probed, giving an appearance of scrutiny. To practitioners of espionage, this represented little difficulty. Secrets were always best kept in open view.

In a minor reorganisation, MI1 had been secretly reconstituted with a brief to undertake specialist surveillance activity of key individuals, corporations or other organisations of significance or interest to Her Majesty's government. It was small, which allowed it to be funded via moveable special projects.

GCHQ facilitated these payments, but did not exclusively control MI1. The other senior security services also used MI1, but none of them controlled it, and MI1, despite its size – a full-time strength of less than fifty staff – was nominally accountable to a responsible minister. This arrangement had been in existence for some twenty years now.

As a career move, Amanda wasn't entirely sure it was a good one. All her work would be deniable, and public acclaim was impossible, but there were a few upsides. It was a position of total trust and it represented a ticket into the very inner circle of the service. Not that she cared about advancement. What she cared about was escaping the endless bureaucracy that had overtaken the service. An end to endless PowerPoint slides vaguely directing crowded, lengthy meetings where every section of every department was represented and had an opinion.

She could afford to be choosy. Financially, her career wasn't that important to her. She would always fall on her feet, and she knew she was attractive. She had also profited from her mistakes. Well, one mistake in particular. A marriage fifteen years ago to a wealthy older man. It hadn't been cynical on her part – she loved and admired him. At first, he loved her too. But any cynicism had been mostly on his part. Like so many wealthy, driven men in late middle age, he was in a hurry and, with women, resisted everything but temptation. It was mostly infatuation and sex, and at first, she had tried hard to keep him. But it was just a numbers game, and eventually he fell in love with one of his conquests and asked for a divorce. It was years before pre-nuptial agreements became an integral part of a wedding ceremony, so Amanda was very well-placed. She was devastated and pretended that the money didn't matter; however, the twenty-million-pound one-off settlement had changed her mind. Well, he could afford it.

It had still taken her a while to restore her self-confidence. But eventually she realised that she was young, attractive and wealthy, with her whole life ahead of her. She had decided that it was time for brains and, building on her Oxbridge first, she returned to full-time study.

This concluded, she took the unusual step of joining the police force and the rest had become history. She was a woman at a time when that was an advantage, and that had helped. Amanda didn't care. She never looked gift horses in the mouth. Anyway, she was where she was on merit.

It had surprised her how enjoyable the work had been, and she found herself intellectually devoted to it. It had also helped that she had been subject to none of the prosaic but grinding challenges that blight many careers. Promotions, office politics and petty grievances passed her by, and if the work interested her, she stayed. And it *had* interested her. Except for the last twelve months.

She had applied for and secured the post she was to begin today. She had only a general idea of what her new department was engaged upon, and this appealed to her. Variety always did.

She had killed a few people in her life. She sometimes thought about them, but it never troubled her. She had been lucky; they had all deserved to die. This wasn't a convenient lie or the narrow thinking of a zealot, just a simple reality. Everyone she had killed had been armed and had been trying to kill her. So that was justice of a sort.

Politically, despite the stereotypical images of those of similar seniority, Amanda was pretty neutral, with almost no dogmatic views and certainly no time for idealism of any sort. She had once been on an anti-war demonstration in her teens, but that had been about that. Nowadays, her philosophy was that Britain was a comparatively decent place and it tried its best, so it needed defending against those, both internal and external, who wished it harm.

She stopped at a crossroads on the edge of the Bloomsbury district and looked up to confirm that she was on the right street. It was home to a long line of brilliant, white-painted terraced townhouses, most occupied as offices, some boutique hotels and very few private dwellings. Number 115 was about halfway along the street, and she skipped up the shallow well-worn steps to a half-glazed front door and pressed on the bell, wondering what lay behind.

Chapter 6

Gerard Gaines wasn't at work today. It wasn't that he was ill or even that he couldn't be bothered: he just had something better to do. He was worried. He had a lot of worrying to do today. At sixty-two years old, the future was coming towards him fast. The clock in the sitting room of his expensive mews house showed 10 a.m., which gave him almost the entire day to worry. He reached for a cigarette that, on inhaling, provoked a violent internal physical reaction. He grimaced then caught a glimpse of his face in a badly placed mirror. It was a discouraging start to the day as vague health, age and mortality fears invaded his thoughts. A subsequent drag of the cigarette drew no reaction, and withdrawing from the death stare of the mirror allowed him to combat and expel these thoughts.

Gaines sat down. His hands were shaking. Time to worry about the business of the day. How had he got into this position? He wasn't sure he wanted to know the answer. It was tough to blame his late parents, both of whom had been minor members of the aristocracy and who, unusually for their class, had been of modest habits and immodest means. He was their only issue and he had inherited the country house, the mews flat and the three million pounds, so it probably wasn't their fault.

He hadn't lacked opportunity or brains, and a genuinely merited double first at Oxford and fast-track civil service promotions had carried him to a senior position where a gold-plated pension and probably a minor honour awaited. Ah, his ex-wife. He could blame her, at least in part. Certainly, she had lived high. That had probably been about manageable, but the two-million-pound divorce settlement with the country house thrown in had changed things. He was a fair man, though, and his ex-wife had loved him for some thirty years while he had quite openly conducted numerous affairs.

He drew on his cigarette. Why had he needed to have so many women? There was no answer, and even if there had been, it didn't matter. That was just how it was, or at least how it had been until now. It was a cliché, but this one was different.

Gaines had never felt like this before, and it scared him. He was sure she felt the same, but even this certainty was worrying. The fear of loss dominated all his waking thoughts. She wasn't the same as the others. She wasn't well off and never had been. She had no interest in money. This was just as well, because most of his money had now gone.

Opportunity had knocked and Gaines had answered. Without thought, and consumed with the thought of making a good life with her, he had walked through the door, which then shut firmly and irrevocably behind him.

He stubbed out his cigarette and considered another, but his deliberations were interrupted by soft steps on the stairs. Her thick, black hair danced carelessly on her face and shoulder. She tried to control it with a vague gesture from her hand. That didn't work, but it didn't matter when you were twenty-seven. She tightened the cord of the robe and sat at his feet, yawning, and let her head fall on his thigh.

Her face beamed up at him. Natasha Gold was in love with him and it felt great. She didn't attempt to explain it either. He was the best part of thirty-five years her senior, but for her, age didn't matter.

She lifted her head and rose. "Want some breakfast?"

"Just a coffee."

He watched as her elegant form moved into the small well-appointed kitchenette and to the coffee machine. It spluttered into action and eventually issued a disappointingly small amount of the black restorative liquid. She returned with two mugs and handed one to him. They did not speak for a minute or so. "Not at work today?" she asked.

He paused for a moment and casually replied, "Oh, I'm meeting Phil Manners at Whitehall for lunch later on." This seemed reasonable. Manners was an undersecretary in the Ministry of Defence, and Gaines had frequent business with him.

"Isn't he on holiday?"

"No, he's just back, I think."

She was staring at him benevolently. He tried without success to calm his shaking hands as he lifted the coffee mug to his lips. She raised an eyebrow but said nothing and looked away.

For a minute they sat in a comfortable silence, then she said, "Right, I'm getting changed and going up to town."

Gaines nodded and watched her as she elegantly ascended the stairs and disappeared into the bedroom.

He was a well-practised liar, both professionally as a member of military intelligence and personally when, at least in the past, covering up affairs. He was very good at lying. Had he done the right thing in lying to her about the lunch date? It was a sloppy lie by his standards, fairly easily uncovered, especially as Natasha also had a day job in military intelligence. He knew deep down that he should have told her the truth; she deserved that, and he knew she would want to help.

He trusted her, certainly, but what if the truth made him lose her? When you were in love, hopelessly, for the first time at the age of sixty-two, that was a risk Gaines was not brave enough to take.

Chapter 7

Jack's villa in Canish was comfortable and he enjoyed his first night. The rooms were large, there was an abundance of books, and when you paid three months up front, the drinks cabinet was full. That was how it was going to remain. Not that he had a "problem", as the experts described these things; he just wanted to get by without it. The cigarettes were another story. The kettle boiled, and he poured a mug of black instant coffee and ventured outside to assess weather prospects for the day. As always, there was a breeze, but the clouds were light and the day mild.

Not that it particularly mattered, for he would likely spend most of the day inside reviewing the work of Clive Moore, his architect. Moore was young and the refurbishment of his hotel was his biggest commission to date. Jack's accountant said it was a risk to use a rookie architect but, given the profile of the entire project, that hardly mattered. Jack had seen something in Moore, and he felt sure he would give everything he had to the project. He would find out soon. He was due to meet Moore at Point End around ten, and it was nine now.

He drifted past the gable of the house and to its front and looked out at nothing in particular. His neighbours were again outside. Jack caught the end of a conversation, which stopped abruptly as one or the other observed him.

Peter Miller blandly acknowledged him as Jack moved to the dividing wall. "Good morning, Mr Edwards."

"Oh, call me Jack."

"Yes, fine. Good day for golf."

Jack agreed that it was. "Yes, but I might not have time today."

Peter Miller didn't exactly force a confidence, but it seemed a natural next step, and Jack explained, "I'm going to Point End to check out some building renovation." Miller nodded and Jack continued. "The hotel."

Miller screwed his eyes in what proved an act of recollection. "Oh, the Lake. Are you doing the building work?"

Jack laughed. "No, commissioning it."

Peter Miller looked surprised but did not respond. Jack thought Miller would soon be saying to his wife, "Here's the fool who's dumping millions into the white elephant at the Point."

Miller was more subtle, and he said to his wife, who had now joined them, "Jack is the man who is developing the Lake Hotel." Suzie betrayed no surprise.

It was at this point Jack realised that everyone within a ten-mile radius of Longtown would know of this venture. He imagined that the consensus of the locals would be "more money than sense", and, in fairness to the wisdom of ordinary folk, they were dead right.

Suzie Miller gave him the middle-class version. "An ambitious project."

Jack agreed, and with this the Millers decided to excuse themselves and drove out.

Jack did likewise. The Maserati screamed into life and he set out for Point End. The road was narrow, with endless blind bends, and the drive wasn't enjoyable. Eventually the road straightened and he slowed as he entered the village. There was a hotel which was today missing tethered horses, a garage with a single exhausted petrol pump, a church hall and a few uninspiring houses.

None of that mattered, because the beauty of Point End lay in the half mile or so beyond the village. A magnificent semi-circular sandy bay with close-attending irregular rocks showcased the ocean. On the south side of the bay lay three small, colourful holiday cottages converted from a former lifeboat house and sheltered by a grassy conical mound known locally as Point End Rock.

As Jack dropped his speed, the road narrowed to single track. He passed and noted with displeasure the proliferation of caravans near the bay, and followed the road alongside the coast. In another four hundred yards, the Lake Hotel crashed into view.

It was so architecturally striking, and all who saw the three-storey white deco building did a double take on first sight. He pulled off the road through an ungated entrance and past a derelict house and, with care, manoeuvred the low-sitting Maserati up a short, winding tarmac ascent.

Moore had at least restored this entrance road, although Jack noted with disappointment that scaffolding still enveloped about half of the building. He stopped at the front of the house and, before he had shut the car door, Moore was there.

Moore was about thirty, athletic and clean-shaven. He had a look that balanced professionalism and enthusiasm, and, although he was young, he accepted that he didn't know everything. Jack shook his hand warmly.

Moore beamed. "So good to see you again, Mr Edwards."

Jack nodded and conducted a short panoramic review. "Lot of activity here, Clive."

"Yes, but we're not behind schedule. The main external stonework is finished. The scaffolding's just for the high windows. Just a few to go. Really, I think you'll be pleased with progress."

His enthusiasm and confident words were infectious, and Jack smiled back. "Okay, let's see."

A circuit of the structure confirmed the good news of the repointed stonework, and internally things looked good also.

Moore led Jack through a restored front entrance and into a central foyer bathed in light with an original staircase restored and room partitioning work very well advanced.

So far, Jack considered his money well spent, and he followed Moore through the ground floor and, in turn, into a bewildering number of expensively furnished rooms. There could be no doubt that Moore had designed and commissioned a triumphant restoration, a view that was confirmed as he led Jack around, all the time beaming and pouring out details of the apartments, fittings and his holistic design philosophy. Jack appreciated the work, but he was running out of ways to express admiration. Luck was at hand, however, as Moore was interrupted. Apparently, there was a dispute with a sub-contractor over a feature window. Moore looked to Jack, who was happy to excuse him.

Chapter 8

Set free from the over-attentive Moore, Jack decided that fresh air and a change of scene were in order. The day was clement with decent visibility, and it was an admirable spot for a stroll, so he left the policies of his property and walked the short distance to the narrow coastal road. It was free of traffic, and he ambled back along it and towards the large, semi-circular bay. He was accompanied only by some high-spirited gulls and eyed indifferently by a seal basking on a rock. He descended some easy ground onto the long and narrow sandy beach. The tide was in, and the sea was calm. He strolled just out of reach of the lapping water, carrying out an unstructured review of the morning's meeting.

There was no doubt that Moore was doing a good job. The restoration and refurbishment would be finished soon. And then what? The house was massive and Jack's family consisted of him alone. He doubted he would spend much time here. There were few commercial possibilities; it would probably be loss-making. He reached the end of the bay with this question unresolved and stopped and looked around. He wasn't ready to go back for part two of the meeting, so he ascended from the bay and pressed on past some small apartments to explore the Point End Rock. It sat at the extreme end of the bay: three hundred feet of basalt extrusion, a proud sentinel extending about a quarter of a mile into the ocean.

He left the easy going of the wet sand for the upland dunes. He stumbled once or twice, and got his boots wet, but after a short walk he arrived at the base of the steep knoll. A challenging scramble over exposed outcrops was possible, but Jack was already breathing more heavily and more frequently than a man of his age should, so he settled for a slow amble round the path which circled the base of the rock.

About halfway round there was a well-placed bench which allowed for uninterrupted ocean views. It was a grand spot and he had it to himself. He sucked in sea air, closed his eyes and let the breeze dance over his face. A hundred feet below, the ocean crashed against the forward defences of the rock. The water would win out one day, but it wasn't going to be today.

Keen to enjoy the rest of the circuit, he forced himself to his feet. He felt like the only man alive – or at least he was for another few seconds, for as he rounded the rock, there was an individual resting near the edge of the path about fifty yards away. Fair enough. It was greedy of him to demand the place all to himself.

As he approached, he identified the sitting figure as a man, middle-aged and casually dressed. His head was bowed and he looked asleep. Through the breeze, the sun was strong and could potentially burn the skin. Sunbathing was bad for you, the tabloids said. The man was impervious to Jack's arrival and Jack wasn't in the mood for a chat. He looked away and determined to continue past the man. But he didn't; a cursory glance noted a large and gaping hole in the side of the prone man's bowed temple. Jack had been right. He was the only man alive in these parts.

Chapter 9

Jack leant forward gingerly for a closer look. The man's head was a mess. The nearside was largely intact, but the offside was not: an untidy mash of brains, bone and blood. The cause of this injury might have been a catastrophic impact against a rock, but Jack knew a gunshot wound when he saw one. And this one had been dealt by a handgun and from close range.

He stood up and suppressed an urge to retch. He conducted a brief scan of the area. There was nothing. No gun and no one. Jack looked back at the man. He had been alive yesterday and now he was dead. In life, the man had been well built and powerful, maybe forty. His clothes were casual, though expensive. At this point Jack's investigation stalled – in part because he had run out of expertise, but mostly because he and the dead man now had company.

She stood about ten yards away and was staring intently at the scene. Jack's first thoughts were of chivalry. This was no place for a woman. He should get her away from the scene. But chivalry was dead, and besides, she didn't look as though she needed saving. She stood immobile, perusing the scene, flicking her eyes between Jack and the dead man. She was young – under thirty. Her light-brown hair was tied back and she was dressed casually. She was good-looking too. Jack was struggling for an opening line, but he needn't have bothered.

In a local but cultured accent she yelled, "Armed police – put your hands on your head."

She looked serious and this was no time for an argument, so Jack did as he was told.

She moved slowly towards him, and the pointing handgun was steady in her hands. It looked like the kind of gun that might have killed the man. She stopped a professional distance from him and, reaching carefully inside her jacket, flashed what he was expected to accept as a police warrant card. Her bona fides established, at least to her own satisfaction, she carried on. He was on his knees now and she rapidly and expertly frisked him. "Where's the gun?"

"I don't have one," Jack said. "Look, I was out for a walk and I found the guy."

"Who are you and what are you doing here?"

"I'm Jack Edwards. I own the hotel." He pointed across the bay, but she didn't look round. A crackling sound emitted from within her jacket and she spoke then listened to a radio.

"Look, I've been meeting my architect, Clive Moore. I came out for a walk."

She reached for her radio again. This done, she said, "Go and sit over there," and indicated a flattish rock. "Slowly." He rose and carefully relocated to the spot indicated. There was a companion rock a few yards away, and for the first time she slightly relaxed her precautions.

"Can I have a cigarette?" Jack asked.

She was clearly one of these anti-smoking types. "How long have you been here?"

"About ten minutes, not longer."

She nodded without indicating acceptance or otherwise. She still looked menacing, but he felt that they had broken the ice. "And who are you?"

Her expression said "none of your fucking business", but she kept things formal. "I'm Detective Inspector Emma Dixon."

She was young for an inspector, but as he regarded her, he decided that she looked more than a quota filler.

"I have colleagues arriving very soon," she said. This proved an accurate forecast, and a few minutes later two uniformed policemen joined their boss.

Policemen were sure getting younger, but they were strong men and they conducted a more vigorous frisk of Jack, confirming he was unarmed. On receiving this assurance, DI Dixon put away her gun and spoke to one of the policemen. He left, and in about five minutes returned with Clive Moore. Moore was a long way out of his comfort zone, but was able, in a short conversation, to confirm Jack's identity.

"I'll be making a statement here," Jack called to Moore. "I'll give you a ring later to re-schedule."

DI Dixon looked at him. Perhaps his assumption of immediate liberty was over-optimistic. By this time, a further team of what looked like forensic experts had arrived and erected a tent over the immediate crime scene.

Unlike the harassed architect, DI Dixon looked well within her comfort zone, and she buzzed between her staff, conducting short meetings and giving directions with assurance. She posted a constable to sit across from Jack. He was fresh-faced, barely out of his teens, and was equally unenthusiastic about Jack's request to smoke, but Dixon evidently overheard and muttered when passing by, "Yes, you may smoke, Mr Edwards."

He took her up on this and felt better. Smoking was bad, but it wasn't bad in response to discovering a dead body and being manhandled by the police. He wanted a brandy too, but he didn't ask. So, he smoked. On the third cigarette, the young policeman was relieved by Dixon.

"I need a full statement."

He nodded and she led him away from the scene and to a squad car. She indicated the back seat and took the front, and they were driven the few miles to Longtown.

The police station at Longtown wasn't extensive and it wasn't beautiful. It consisted of a drab, two-storey domestic building with an abutting flat-roofed extension. Jack wasn't under arrest, but he wasn't quite free yet. Officially, he was making a voluntary statement. Not that he had much more to tell. He followed Dixon through the front door of the house and past a crude reception area into what he imagined was the extended area. It consisted of an open space populated by a single, disinterested computer user and a door which led to an interview area.

Jack accepted DI Dixon's invitation to sit on an uncomfortable plastic chair while she sat opposite. She dismissed her accompanying constable. "Would you like a coffee, Mr Edwards?"

He nodded and she spent a minute or so preparing the drinks. He wondered how she had known he took it black and sugarless. Well, she *was* a detective. She removed her jacket, and from a drawer in the well-used desk retrieved a pen and a pad of paper. She looked at him with piercing blue eyes. "Right – just tell me again why and when you were at the rock today."

Jack told her.

"Did you know the dead man?"

"No, I am an occasional visitor here. I don't know anybody."

"Why did you buy the hotel?" She added wistfully, "A strange purchase."

He agreed that it was. "To be honest, I'm not sure." It wasn't much of an answer, but it was true. He didn't add to his answer. It would have struck the wrong tone to tell her that he had bought it on a whim – because he could afford to.

She was perceptive, though. "Because you can?"

He left that alone.

The constable knocked and entered. "Do you have any objection to providing fingerprints and a DNA sample?" Dixon asked.

Jack did, but went along with it and the constable undertook the exercise and left.

"Thank you, Mr Edwards. This will obviously help us to eliminate you from our enquiries as soon as possible."

He knew a little about these procedures but said nothing. Before the conversation could continue, the constable returned and beckoned Dixon to join him. She excused herself. He sipped the instant coffee and waited. This time, the delay must have been at least twenty minutes. When she returned, she looked quite serious. He was innocent, but, being a middle-class Scottish guy, the police still scared him.

Dixon cocked her head and rested it on her hand. "Sorry for the wait. I was getting a bit of feedback on your prints and now the DNA sample. Obviously, we have not yet gathered any forensic evidence from the victim or the scene. When we do, we will, hopefully, be able to clear you."

She looked as if she did hope for this, which was a help. She looked at him carefully. "However, when we run your records, we find that you are 'classified', Mr Edwards. Now why would that be?"

In truth, he wasn't that sure, but he imagined it was something to do with his connection with his friend and full-time spook, Amanda Barratt. He made to answer but he wasn't sure how to. Vaguely, he remembered he had once signed the Official Secrets Act. He didn't know what to do or to say, so he handed Dixon his phone.

"If you call this number, Amanda Barratt will be able to help."

"Who is she?"

Jack couldn't really describe Amanda, and he had no idea what her current job was. "Look, I'm not an expert at this sort of thing. If you phone Miss Barratt she will, I'm sure, explain. She's in your line of work – a policewoman I think."

Jack was there to answer questions and not give directions. Dixon dialled the number. He had been out of luck so far today, but now things were looking up. The phone was answered quickly.

Dixon announced herself and listened to a longer response. Imperceptibly, she sat up a little taller in her seat.

Appraising Jack, she said, "About forty, five feet eleven, maybe thirteen stone, Caucasian, brown eyes." She handed the phone to Jack.

Amanda wasn't annoyed, but she had been friendlier. He explained the position, and, without further small talk, she instructed him to return the mobile. He did what he was told. Being bossed around by female authority figures was to be his lot today, and he waited a further five minutes as the arbiters of his fate chatted on.

The call ended with what was almost a laugh from Dixon, which he supposed was a good sign. She handed back his phone. "Okay, just sign this statement and then you can go. We may want to speak to you again."

He let out a low but embarrassing sigh of relief. He seemed to be off the hook, so he allowed himself a brief, less formal, appraisal of Dixon. She was certainly attractive, although understated. He liked her. She looked at him and he quickly looked away.

"If you wait a minute, I'll arrange to get you back to your hotel."

He was disappointed when she returned with the young constable – he would have preferred to be driven by her. Even if that didn't happen, Jack hoped that he would see Emma Dixon again – hopefully in less formal circumstances.

Chapter 10

Jack awoke early the next morning in the villa at Canish and got out of bed as if he had a purpose. It wasn't the hotel that was on his mind. Any normal person would have suffered a reaction of disgust and personal upset to yesterday's events, but he didn't feel all that much. He had seen a few dead bodies now in his life, and once you got used to the first one, especially if it was someone you had loved, you changed forever.

He wanted to phone Amanda, but he decided on a breakfast of coffee and cigarettes first. He hadn't seen her for a while. Why? At times it seemed obvious that she was the woman for him. About the same age, attractive, strong and intelligent. And she quite liked him too. Why weren't they together? He couldn't find an answer. He had another cigarette and turned on the radio. He wasn't in the mood for inane political chat. Political events short of full-scale revolution were of no real interest to someone as wealthy as he was. The revolution wasn't going to start today, so he switched to classical music and turned his mind dispassionately to yesterday's events.

He started respectfully, by reminding himself that the dead man would be mourned by someone. This was true, but there was no point pretending that it affected him deeply, so he thought more forensically about the murder. It could have been suicide, of course. The gunshot was certainly delivered at close quarters. Set against that, surely the gun would have lain alongside if it had been suicide. Perhaps he had overlooked it, but he thought not. Thrown into the lapping ocean by an unknown hand seemed much more likely. What he was sure of was that the wound was from a handgun. They were much rarer in Scotland now after Dunblane, and surely a suicide would use a shotgun or rifle, both of which were comparatively abundant in this remote rural area.

He cut short his musings; he needed more information. He doubted he would get it. But this assumption proved false when, on answering a loud knock, Jack found Inspector Emma Dixon at his front door. This time, he was more pleased than anxious, and she was unaccompanied. He invited her in and led her through to the kitchen, indicating a breakfast bar seat. She accepted a better-quality coffee than she had blended yesterday and displayed no obvious reaction to his lighting a cigarette. It was a good start.

She started reasonably formally, but this time it was mostly good news – at least for Jack. "First things first. You are in the clear, I think."

He tilted his head. "You think?"

"Well, Moore confirms your timings. The man was killed about one to two hours before you finished meeting with Mr Moore. Also, there is no trace evidence."

He nodded. "Well, there wouldn't be. I never touched the body."

"Training?" she enquired, but he made no reply, so she went on. "Here's a bit of background."

He wondered why she was telling him this, but decided just to listen.

"The deceased was a local, name of Bobby Lennon. He was a long-time resident and well known in the area." Her face hardened. "Well known, but not well liked."

Jack figured that this was quite often true of murder victims, but said nothing.

Instead, he offered her another coffee, which she accepted. More surprisingly, she accepted his offer of a cigarette.

"Lennon was actually a neighbour of yours. He had a villa a couple of doors down. The first one as you come into the village. He lived there with his partner – a woman called Val Fraser."

"Long term?" Jack enquired.

"Yes, about ten or so years. No kids."

It was usually someone close to the victim who committed the murder. "How did they get on?"

"Okay, as far as I know," Emma said neutrally.

Jack decided to chuck in one of his ideas. "Are you sure it wasn't a suicide? I mean, did you find a gun?"

She shook her head. "No, we didn't. Besides, Bobby Lennon wasn't the type, in my opinion. He was in his forties and in good condition. He was retired from the army and had an interest in a local building firm. He was quite well off."

Jack took a drag of his cigarette. "Not well liked, you said."

Emma flicked her short, light-brown hair off her face, "A loudmouth and a show-off." She added, with Presbyterian censure, "Very interested in women."

Jack nodded a bit. He used to be interested in women as well, but it didn't seem the time to mention it.

"Usually other men's wives."

Irrespective of any moral judgements, Jack was sure that this sort of behaviour would certainly make real enemies in these parts. Not like a city, where folks were fishing in a very large pond. Whether this amounted to a motive for murder was another thing.

She made no further comment on this either, but carried on with her briefing. "Lennon was very friendly with your neighbours on the other side."

Jack at least knew them. "I met them yesterday. Suzie and Peter Miller. They seemed okay."

"Yes, nice people."

"I wouldn't have thought that they'd have much in common with the sort of man you describe. However, I don't know them at all."

"There used to be a big NATO airbase here and Lennon and the Millers both worked there," Emma said.

Jack nodded. "Why are you telling me all this?"

"Come on, you can help me, I think. Would you come down to Point End with me?"

He had nothing better to do, and both Emma and the case were interesting – certainly more interesting than the hotel.

He thought about offering to take the Maserati to Point End with the twin aims of impressing her and being able to smoke, but he decided not to offer. She was on duty, and she might need the facilities his civilian vehicle lacked. He jumped into the passenger seat of her unmarked car.

It was strange, but you could always tell if a car was owned by a woman. They were just cleaner and they smelled better. He pushed the seat back, relaxed and enjoyed being driven.

They chatted easily, and the journey was over too soon for Jack. To his surprise, Emma did not direct the car towards the murder scene but drove round the point for a mile or so before pulling into a rough car park adjacent to another large sandy bay. This time, the tide was about half a mile out, and the graduated yellow shading made it an attractive sight. It was also deserted, and he followed Emma as she made her way through some low-lying dunes and onto the beach. He wondered why he was here, but he didn't ask and she made no effort to explain; but an explanation arrived soon and from above. Not a divine intervention, but from a remote and noisy black shape which gradually revealed itself as a helicopter. A few minutes later it landed on the wet sand. A figure emerged and moved towards them.

Emma bade Jack stay and began to walk towards the figure. It was impossible to identify the visitor, but Jack knew it would be Amanda. The women came together and for several minutes were deep in conversation. Their conference concluded, they joined him. Amanda was about ten years older than Emma, but it was no disadvantage. She was wearing a knee-length heavy waxed coat, but it didn't matter what she wore. The breeze whipped her hair irregularly around her head. She pushed it away and said, with a suspicion of a smile, "Hello, Jack." She moved a step towards him and put her arms around his neck and gave him a squeeze and an informal kiss. Then she snapped into business mode.

"I have explained to Detective Inspector Dixon who you are, who I am and that you are occasionally an asset, of sorts, to HM Government. I have asked Detective Inspector Dixon if she would accommodate me by including you in her investigation."

This caught him by surprise. He was grateful to her and her offices for vouching for him, but could hardly see why this should develop into an active role.

Amanda seemed to read his expression. "Just to put you in the picture, Jack, Bobby Lennon was, in the past, also an asset of my department. Before my time, of course."

"What department is that?"

"A new one. I've just taken it over. Anyway, Lennon hasn't worked for us for years, but we like to know when something unfortunate happens to our pensioners."

Jack let this go. As always when Amanda involved him in her affairs, he initially resented her assumption that he could be deployed without consultation, but he conceded to himself that action was an attraction. He just nodded. "What do you want me to do?"

"Just tag along with Detective Inspector Dixon and don't make a nuisance of yourself. It's her case. Just give me a ring as you go forward." She leant in towards him. "Oh, and remember, we have no secrets from the police." She had the honesty to add, "For the time being."

He looked at Emma. Local actors often resented the interposing of state power in their affairs, but Emma was either very passive or very ambitious and seemed entirely comfortable with this state of affairs. Perhaps she was flattered that a head of a directorate had flown here just to see her but, whatever the reason, the conference was over, and Amanda gave Jack another hug and retraced her steps to the chopper.

Jack and Emma watched her in silence until the helicopter was airborne.

"Come on, let's get started," Emma said.

Chapter 11

Emma wasn't hanging around. On the return journey she drove at a speed only a local dared. She didn't turn off at Canish, however, but drove into town and pulled up in the car park of a modern-looking set of commercial units.

"We are going to see Adam Jardine. He's local, got a successful business. His older brother is one of the most successful businessmen in the area. He was in the army and used to be a good friend of Lennon. Lennon owned a share in his business. By all accounts, the friendship was over some time ago and the relationship went bad. Doubt he will be upset. Let's see. Oh, and just let me do the talking."

Jack followed her into the main office. Jardine was in and they were shown straight through. He looked up from a disorganised pile of architectural drawings. and smiled pleasantly. "Hi, Emma."

Jack had forgotten that everyone knew everyone in Longtown. Jardine's smile receded as he eyed Jack.

"This is Jack Edwards." Emma didn't give him a title, but Jardine didn't seem interested. "You can guess why I'm here, Adam."

Jardine nodded.

"When did you last see him?"

"Yesterday morning, about nine."

"What about?"

"Just a business meeting. You know he had a share of the business?"

"Yes."

Jardine seemed a pretty straightforward guy and, without being prompted, added, "To be honest, Emma, it wasn't a great meeting. We have been, er, negotiating the sale of his shares."

"And how long was the meeting?"

"About fifteen minutes, not more."

"Anything different about him?"

Jardine said sadly, "No, he was just the same."

"Did he say where he was going?" Emma asked.

"Nope."

"And what about you, Adam? Where were you yesterday after the meeting?"

"I was here for about another half an hour and then up to the site. I was with dozens of men and contractors until about seven at night."

"You never left the site?"

"Not until seven in the evening," Jardine said.

"Give me a few names," Emma said. "Write them down. I'll need to check, of course."

Adam Jardine picked up a pen and a scrap of paper and scribbled.

Emma inspected the note. "Thanks. Have you any idea who might have killed him?"

"Well, you know as well as I do that Bobby wasn't popular. He had a few enemies."

Emma nodded again.

Jack thought Jardine seemed genuine enough. Besides, he didn't look the type. The man Jack had stumbled upon yesterday had a part of his head missing, it was true, but before that he had been a much more powerful man than Jardine. Jardine was about forty and a big man, but he was puffy and didn't look up for the task.

"You were in the army with Bobby?" Emma asked him.

"Yes, but just for a few years. The army wasn't for me. Bought myself out."

"Were you ever at the airbase?"

"No, never."

"You got a gun, Adam?"

"Well a shotgun, but you know about that. It's all licensed. Nothing else."

Emma seemed finished and she got up. She had one more question. "Have you seen Val recently?"

Jardine face reddened. "No ... er ... well ... once, in town the other day. In the passing. I don't think she saw me. We didn't talk."

Emma thanked him and she and Jack left.

Back in the car, Jack asked, "Who's Val?"

"She's Lennon's partner. Let's go and see her."

The drive was a mere five minutes and they didn't talk much during the journey. As she had told him, Lennon's villa was a couple of units short of his rental villa. It was of similar size and construction.

Val Fraser was about forty, and her unkempt blonde hair and lined face told of a difficult night. She invited them inside without a word.

The house was well kept and the furniture was expensive and modern, although not to Jack's taste. She led them through to a sitting room and sat down in a black leather armchair. She lit a cigarette and reached for a chunky tumbler sitting on an adjacent table. She didn't offer them a drink, nor bother with an insincere apology for drinking in the middle of the day.

Emma regarded her for a moment as if looking for a suitable opening. She went for a platitudinous expression of regret, which Val Fraser accepted with a nod. "Obviously we have to get as much information as possible, Val, so can I get started?" Val nodded again and took a long mouthful of her drink.

"When did you last see Bobby?"

"At breakfast yesterday morning. He went into town about half past eight."

"Why was he going to town?" Emma asked.

"I don't know. Why would he tell me? And I didn't ask," Val added.

It was already clear that this relationship was no love job.

"Did he seem different?" Emma said.

Val took another slug of the clear drink. "No."

"Did Bobby have a gun?"

"Yes, I think he still had his old service pistol, but I haven't seen it for years."

Emma said, "And how have things been between you and Bobby recently?"

Val emitted a silent laugh and looked hard at Emma. "Pretty much living separate lives for the last year or two, but of course you know that, Emma."

Emma didn't react to this remark. "Where were you yesterday?"

"I tidied up a bit here and went to the stables."

"For how long?"

Val considered. "I got back here about three o'clock, I think."

"Yes, we called for you about two o'clock and you were out."

It was pretty light questioning, but Jack supposed that it was very early on in the investigation. Val rose and helped herself to another drink, again ignoring her guests.

It was time he got into the action. "Do you mind if I smoke?"

Val shrugged. "I didn't know policemen smoked on duty."

"Mr Edwards isn't a policeman, Val."

Val raised an eyebrow. Jack was interested to hear Emma's description of what he was too.

"Mr Edwards is from the Home Office." Emma added unconvincingly, "He happened to be in the area and is assisting."

Val made the link. "Home Office? It's over ten years since Bobby was in the agency."

Emma brushed over this. "Now, Val, Bobby wasn't very popular. Has anything happened recently that I need to know? Any problems with anyone in particular?"

Val gave a hollow laugh. "Not popular," she repeated slowly. "That's a fucking understatement, Emma. He wasn't even popular in his own home. Look, I have no idea who killed him, it could have been anyone."

"You will need to formally identify him," Emma said.

Val shrugged. "Let me know when."

"Okay, I'll be in touch. That's all for now."

Emma and Jack got up but Val didn't, and they saw themselves out. There was a long way to go, but one key thing was obvious. The period of mourning in Lennon's former home was now at an end – if it had ever even started.

Chapter 12

Jack returned to the car and waited, but Emma didn't unlock it. "We'll leave it here." He followed as she walked past Jack's villa to the door of his neighbours. They were at home, and Peter Miller led Jack and Emma inside. The room was similar in dimensions to Val Fraser's living room but was more lightly and tastefully decorated. There were books, a lot of them, and they improved the room, as did the absence of a large-screen television.

Suzie Miller was in also and was sitting comfortably at the end of an attractive sofa, reading a book. She was dressed casually and was reading with half-framed glasses, which she removed as they arrived.

"Sit down, please," Peter said and indicated a sofa opposite. He sat alongside his wife. She put down her book and the Millers looked puzzled.

"This is Jack Edwards, from the Home Office," Emma said again. He had a title now. "I believe you have already met."

The Millers nodded.

"Obviously you know about Bobby Lennon? We are just making preliminary enquiries. We'll be talking to all the neighbours."

They nodded in unison again. Emma evidently didn't know the Millers as well as she knew Val Fraser. "You moved to Canish ten years ago?"

"Twelve," Peter corrected.

"And you both worked at the airbase?"

Peter was the spokesman. "Suzie worked at the base, but although I spent a lot of time there, I worked there as a contractor."

"For what sort of company?"

"An IT communications company."

"So, you have lived here about twelve years?"

"Yes, I moved down then. Suzie, of course, is a native."

Emma nodded, and Jack was emboldened now. A cigarette in this pristine house would never be allowed, so he asked a question. "What work did you do at the base, Mrs Miller?"

"Just general administrative work, gathering and compiling information."

Jack was on a roll. "And that's how you two met?"

The Millers looked at each other and beamed a little. They both said, "Yes." There was certainly more love in this house. Suzie had broken off the glance, but her husband was still beaming at her. Jack wondered whether her husband was more in love than she was. He was at least twenty years older than her, and he looked it. Had they ever been mistaken for father and daughter? It was possible.

"I understand that you were quite friendly with Bobby and Val," Emma said. "And, of course, you worked with Val at the airbase, Suzie."

"Yes, but not in the same department."

Peter Miller took the lead again. "Yes, we were quite close for a while, but that was a good few years ago. In the last couple of years not so much."

"Why?" Jack asked.

Peter shrugged. "No reason, really – we were all a bit younger and liked to go out a lot. Nothing happened, really. We just didn't go out so much. We wanted to do different things, had different interests."

"What about you and Val?" Emma asked Suzie.

"Yes, I still see her quite often. I mean, we're neighbours and she is an old friend."

Emma nodded. "What about Bobby – did you fall out with him?"

Jack noted that it was unclear whether the question was directed to them collectively or to Suzie particularly.

The Millers looked at each other before Peter Miller reassumed the role of spokesman. "Well, Bobby was, well, Bobby." He added, stiffly, "It would be fair to say that, over time, we found his company less interesting. There was no fall out. Nothing specific."

"When did you last see him?"

"A week or so ago."

This time, Emma didn't accept a collective answer. "What about you, Suzie?"

She flushed a little and Peter Miller's features tightened. "Oh, a couple of days ago. I went to see Val for a coffee."

"Did either of you see him yesterday?"

They both shook their heads.

Emma then came to, what Jack now recognised as, her closing questions. It emerged that Peter Miller had been golfing from late morning to the late afternoon while Suzie had been at home for most of the day, save for an hour or so in the late morning when she had shopped.

"Were you playing golf with anyone?"

"No, on my own."

Suzie could remember meeting no one she knew. Neither were airtight alibis.

They both disclaimed any knowledge of who might want Lennon dead, and at this stage there was nothing else to say. Emma thanked them both, and she and Jack left and made their way back to the car.

A thought that had been percolating in Jack's mind finally found its voice. "Has Suzie Miller had an affair with Lennon?"

Emma turned and looked at him. "Why would you ask that?"

"I've no idea, to be honest."

She paused for a moment and then said, "I don't know, but they say so."

The Millers had suddenly become interesting.

Chapter 13

In the heart of central London, Gerard Gaines sat in his old-fashioned, cavernous attic office. The furniture was old but of a higher specification than allowed nowadays by government departments. It was the best office in the building, which was fair enough as he had been acting head of MI1 for the last four years. He had hoped that he might continue in that role until retirement, but this was not to be.

He had not yet met Amanda Barratt, but he had heard about her. A new broom on the fast track. She would be spot on with gender and racial issues and, no doubt, a fierce advocate of the newest and most modern methods.

That might be all right. He was sure he could adapt. More concerning was *why* she was here. MI1 was a strategically insignificant outpost of the intelligence estate, and he knew of no planned future expansion of the department's role. Its methods had largely been replaced by satellite-based mass surveillance techniques. Why would a high-flying appointee land here?

Gaines resumed his more immediate and prosaic personal worries. It was true that he might clear his feet if he sold the Cookham cottage, but it would be tight. And then what? Was Natasha the kind of girl who would be happy living on a government pension? Maybe at first, but he wasn't confident.

By any standards, Gaines had been born with many advantages, and he had never found a problem that he couldn't deal with. This was the biggest problem of his life, and it was tough to handle one's biggest crisis at sixty, especially after finding love for the first time. On the credit side he was, theoretically, in the clear, and it was not certain that things would develop unfavourably. Indeed, he had been reassured that everything was under control, but that reassurance came from David Preece, and Gaines didn't trust Preece.

It was going to take more than clichés to calm Gaines. Lennon's murder would be seen as a local affair, though, and this rallied him. Hopefully the meeting would settle things. Either way, he could not shake his analysis that his dog days were over. Amanda Barratt was twenty years younger than him and she was his boss. Her network was not his network. He was out of the loop professionally, and out of his depth personally. He was yesterday's man, and he felt it.

Chapter 14

David Preece wasn't changing his job today, but that didn't matter. He loved his work. From his substantial and palatial office in the City of London, he looked outside and noted with indifference that the rain had stopped. He swivelled his chair round and extended his legs lazily under the length of his massive rosewood desk.

Beyond the desk, and covering many square metres, the rectangular, high-ceilinged room was opulently appointed. The various items of furniture had been selected individually from a large budget supported by the services of an in-house designer. He particularly liked the Le Corbusier chairs that were perfectly arranged around the coffee table. They, of course, were much copied, and versions could be found in any office or workaday office catalogues. The difference here was that they were *original* Le Corbusier chairs.

Preece scanned the remainder of the office, noting the Marcel Breuer and Ludwig Mies van der Rohe pieces. He wondered idly for a moment whether the authenticity of the furniture was at odds with the authenticity of his work as a partner, albeit a junior one, in a global hedge fund. He dismissed the thought. Money came in and, somehow, more was generated and returned with quite a lot retained as commission. How it was generated was never all that clear, but he had never really cared.

Nominally, Preece had an executive job, but the bland professionals who ran the operation never asked him to execute anything. His duties could only be described as light. Client meetings, a board meeting once a quarter, a number of city functions, an occasional speech, and his name on the letterhead were the extent of his commitment. All this was easy enough. There were times when he reflected that he was wasting his life. These reflections were fewer now, but they were something to do while he waited for his next appointment. Today's business consisted of a lunch date with a Middle Eastern businessman with a fortune to invest. Preece didn't know much about investment strategies, but he did know a bit about Middle East protocol from his time as a government minister, so he was confident.

He turned his head and gazed out of the window, inwardly laughing at the hectic activity below from worker ants clasping their overpriced coffees and rushing into innumerable offices. Many of them would be convinced that they were doing something important. He knew that mostly they weren't. Securing control of billions of dollars and ensuring it flowed globally was important. Oh, the little people. Out of control and powerless to affect even their own lives; why couldn't they see that?

To be fair, it had taken him a little while. As a radical student, he too believed that the route to power was through ideology and action. When those had failed, he had convinced himself that a career as a democratic politician was the best route to power, so he worked hard and got himself elected to Parliament. The traditions and rituals of the Palace of Westminster thrilled and overwhelmed him for a few months, but after that he didn't feel too powerful as an MP either. Surely senior political office would do it? He tried hard to keep his nose clean, voted obediently in the lobby, sold out a few causes, and with a sharp dress sense, projected an image of loyalty and competence.

Undersecretary in the Ministry of Defence wasn't exactly high office, but when he eventually realised that military power, either threatened or deployed, controlled the globe, he recognised that, at last, he was somewhere where influence made a difference and high-powered connections could be established. The UK wasn't the military power it had been in the past, but it was far from insignificant and its influence remained surprisingly wide. Although there was little risk of the country being invaded, war and the weapons of war were a key UK industry.

The work in the Ministry had also introduced Preece to the world of real power. A world of regime change and loveless and selfish temporary, strategic alliances. He now knew many of the world's biggest criminals. Most were personally charming, and they weren't exclusively based in the third world.

He wondered why he didn't feel guilty. He asked himself that quite frequently and he always came up with the same answer. He was a hollow man, living exclusively for himself and for the moment. Why not? God was dead – or perhaps on a long-term break. What else was there other than one's self?

This realisation, and his acceptance of it, had been a great stroke of luck, for once you knew what you were, there was pretty much nothing you wouldn't do. There had been few costs thus far – except for the failure of a loveless and childless marriage – and David Preece, well off and well connected, had an excellent present, which he fully intended to enjoy.

Bored with looking out of the window, he rose and wandered around his office, stopping only to positively review his appearance in a full-length mirror. Tall, handsome and having just gained his middle age – Preece was a happy man. The telephone rang and drew him back to his desk. He acknowledged the caller airily and then vaguely took in the first four sentences from the receiver.

Both the caller and the words demanded attention, and after a further minute, Preece replaced the handset and contemplated a less rosy future.

He picked up a coat, rejected it and made his way out of his office. The rays of the summer sun were still strong, and the Russell

Square park was a pleasant place to be on a late summer afternoon. It was busy with workers mostly heading off early, but he found a bench withdrawn from the main pathway.

He half-closed his eyes and enjoyed the rays of the sun. The noise of the traffic could not be completely eliminated, but the closely growing trees and shrubs did a good job, and in his ears the sound of the bird chatter held its own. There were no nightingales, but there were starlings, sparrows and a couple of small but noisy wrens. The smells were good too, with plants open for business to a number of busy bees. Time was really the only thing that mattered, and this time the world was in perfect order.

Imperfection was restored a few seconds later as, in response to a gathering sound of feet on gravel, Preece opened his eyes and observed the unmistakeable gait of Gerard Gaines moving towards him. Gaines moved like an old man and, as he neared, Preece could see that Gaines *looked* like an old man. They said he had a lover who was in her twenties, but Preece doubted that very much.

Gaines looked around conspiratorially before inspecting the bench and then cautiously risking his expensive suit on it. The bench was wide and Gaines kept his distance. At close quarters, he didn't look any better. Preece watched as his trembling hands eventually lit a cigarette. Worse, his face had gone beyond craggy and could be accurately described as fallen. Preece knew that a chain was only as strong as its weakest link, and Gaines was, undoubtedly, that link.

Gaines had asked for this meeting, but it was risky and unnecessary. There was, it was true, a reasonable backstory for the two men having a relationship and a meeting. They had worked together, albeit briefly, when Preece was in government, although that had been about a decade ago. Nevertheless, a friendship of sorts had been formed.

Preece knew Gaines needed reassurance, and so it proved. In faltering tones, Gaines asked, "Did you hear about Lennon?"

"Yes, I heard, but you're worrying about nothing, Gerard. I told you that on the phone. Lennon was reckless. He would try a saint."

"Well, yes. You *are* convinced it's a local affair?"

Preece looked at him quizzically. "Of course, what else?"

"I don't know." Gaines added, "Where does it leave the unit?"

"Well, inaction would seem to be indicated at this stage."

That was unarguable, so Gaines moved on to another concern. "You know I have a new boss? Amanda Barratt."

"Yes, I know." Preece instantly realised he'd made a mistake.

Gaines looked up sharply. "How do you know that?"

Preece couldn't tell Gaines the whole truth. "I just heard, think an old colleague mentioned it. But I don't know anything about her. It's nothing to worry about. She's just a token quota appointment. She'll be on her way in six months. Just work experience for a high-flyer."

"Maybe, what else have you heard?"

"Nothing. Honestly, Gerald, I really can't see what's bothering you."

The inconclusive meeting seemed to have run its course. Gaines looked grey and continued to smoke. He seemed not to have anything else to say, and his chin sat slumped on his chest.

Preece patted his arm. "Nothing to worry about, Gerard. I need to go now."

He rose, wondering whether he had reassured Gaines, but a look over his shoulder provided an answer – the sight of a sixty-year-old man talking softly to himself represented a comprehensive failure.

Chapter 15

It was Amanda's third day as director of MI1. After a largely wasted first day when there had been no key staff in the office, she had spent day two on a helicopter ride to and from Scotland. It had been good to see Jack, but it was now time for real work.

She remembered the passcode and went through the outer door. From an opening in the frosted glazing, a voice called out, "Morning, ma'am."

"Morning," she shouted back without turning.

The voice clicked open the door ahead and she made her way up broad, lino-covered stairs to the working floors of the directorate. Most of the work was carried out on the first floor. The once well-appointed individual apartments of the Georgian terrace had been levelled and a 1970s-style renovation had created a single open-plan area, with two-part glass-fronted offices at the far wall.

Four of the dozen or so desks in the open-plan area were taken, three of them by technical-looking men who were absorbed in the reconstruction of a mechanical device. So much for modern technology. They looked but didn't acknowledge her. She went through the door in the partition marked "Director" and re-acquainted herself with the desk she had met for about ten minutes yesterday.

Absence hadn't made the heart grow fonder. The office was deceptively large, but that was about the only good point. The desk, conference table and cabinets were functional, if you liked vintage furniture. The cheap black seat behind the desk was more modern but was in worse condition and was short of a castor. MI1 was an old department, and it smelled old.

Amanda threw her briefcase and coat on the table, sat cautiously on her desk chair and surveyed her fiefdom. At least there was a window to look out of, and through its three large, dirty panes it flooded the office with daylight, exposing every blemish and dust particle in the room. She got off the seat carefully and walked to the window. Below sat a long and narrow garden area. Someone obviously had made sure it was well tended, and it was an attractive space in the madness of central London.

Sitting in the garden wasn't really for today, so she moved her attention to a table in front of the window. It was home to the only concession to the twenty-first century: a newish-looking coffee machine sat alongside what seemed to be a full set of ingredients. Amanda had a go at the machine, hitting a few buttons on a trial and error basis. After a couple of false starts and a couple of swear words, she stood back and looked at the machine. As she considered the problem, a better answer arrived in the shape of a tall, good-looking man, under the age of thirty, who knocked and entered.

"Let me do that, ma'am," he said in a southern accent that might have been his own.

She stood aside and watched as, with long elegant hands and manicured nails, he hit the right buttons and laid two mugs in the right place.

She looked at him. His black hair was expensively styled, and his strong jaw, designer stubble and near black eyes completed a face that was as attractive as his hands. His clothes unexceptional – suit trousers and a white shirt with a single button undone – but they looked good on his slim muscular frame and were clearly designed by names that most people had heard of.

He extended his hand. "Julian Johns, ma'am. I'm the director's assistant." In Amanda's business, that position involved a bit more than making the coffee. There was administration and there were some low chores, but there was also access – both to senior people and to highly classified material. It was a position that many high-flyers had been fast tracked onto, and, from there, further on.

The coffee machine spluttered to an end. She handed him a coffee and invited him to sit at the modestly sized conference table. There were only four seats around it and he selected one alongside her.

"Okay, Julian – tell me all about MI1."

Julian Johns took a mouthful of coffee. "I've been here about a year as assistant."

"From where?" Amanda interrupted.

"Oh, various jobs in the City after university."

"So why the Intelligence Services?"

"It's worthwhile . . . essential. I believe in this country."

It wasn't a bad answer, but it was never an answer Amanda liked. She was a pragmatist, not an ideologue, and she didn't like ideologues.

"Obviously one of my briefs here is to undertake a review of the continuing relevance of this department. There will be those who are inclined to close it down, amalgamate it with GCHQ."

Johns nodded. "Yes, I can see how, economically, there might be a case for that, but set against that there are, from time to time, jobs which are best done at arm's length."

Amanda was sceptical. "Are there skills and expertise here that are unique?"

He considered. "There are, but the improvement in technology has reduced our edge. But we are invisible."

Amanda nodded and changed the subject. "And what about *you*? Do you not find it a bit slow here?"

He was quite open in response. "Yes, but seeing how a directorate works and being in a highish position is interesting. I get to work and talk with other directors' assistants – see what's going on at the top and how it all works." He added cheerfully, "To be frank, I don't think I'd want to stay here until retirement, but it's great experience for me."

"And your next move?"

He smiled easily. "Oh, nothing specific – really anything that's interesting and, of course, useful and worthwhile."

"What worthwhile things are we doing at the moment?" Amanda asked.

"Wait a minute." Johns left the office and returned a few seconds later with a handful of files, which he placed on the table.

The active reports were unexciting, consisting of a few updates on an interminable IT project as well as status reports on various intelligence assessment exercises which Amanda suspected had been commissioned elsewhere.

"Is that it?"

"Yes, we have no active operations at present. However, they do happen from time to time."

No doubt that was true, but a workload as light as this with only vague responsibilities was surely not long for the Whitehall world.

Amanda looked at Johns. "Where are you from?"

His features tightened a little. It seemed less favoured ground. "Balford."

She knew where that was, but she asked him anyway.

He laughed. "North Lancashire. A one, or perhaps, two-horse town."

She didn't force the issue. It was clear that Johns had left there a long time ago and was never going back.

She leant towards him. "Right, tell me about the people – who's able, who's good, who's no good."

Julian Johns shrugged. "Well, Gerard. Gerard Gaines has been acting head for years. Tremendous amount of experience, of course, goes way back."

"I haven't met him yet. Where's his office, the one next to mine?"

"No, he has the attic floor above. They extended into it about ten years ago. It's a big space."

"And do you know where Mr Gaines is?" Amanda asked. "I was hoping to have spoken to him by now."

"Not sure, I think he was on holiday for a couple of days - although he was in today for an hour or so. Do you want his phone number?"

Amanda considered. "No, I'd rather see him face to face for a first meeting."

Johns apparently had nothing else to say about Gaines. "Natasha Gold, she's the head of HR here. She's about my age. Efficient and able, I would say."

Johns stopped and looked at Amanda. She held his gaze for a moment, inviting further details, but it seemed that he had nothing much more to say. Why?

"Well, I'm going to have to meet them all," she said.

Johns seemed to jump at the chance to get off the subject. "Yes, of course, I'll ask Natasha to come in. She'll be able to tell you where Gerard is. Do you want to see her now?"

Amanda wasn't really finished, but Johns seemed to be.

"Yes, see if she's around."

He left, and a few seconds later there was a confident knock on the door. Natasha Gold entered and, responding to Amanda's gesture, sat down on the seat recently vacated by Julian Johns.

Natasha Gold was about the same age and nearly as good-looking as Johns. She moved well and sat down confidently with a single file under her arm. She offered Amanda her hand and introduced herself, handed her a couple of sheets of paper and started talking in confident, prepared tones. In about fifteen minutes, Natasha Gold had summarised every member of the directorate. Amanda groaned inwardly as she described a collection of staff either coasting to retirement or with outdated skills.

Natasha looked at Amanda with an expression close to pity.

Amanda laughed. "Not very encouraging. However, we're here to change all this."

Natasha brightened. She nodded with enthusiasm.

Amanda smiled back more confidently than she felt. This was going to be a challenge, but on the plus side, this directorate, so insignificant and outdated, seemed to have a couple of rising stars.

Chapter 16

Natasha Gold had only met her new boss briefly, but already she was impressed. Amanda Barratt represented almost everything Natasha wanted to be in ten years' time. That she was a woman was useful, and she was certainly a looker. These things helped, but what was even more useful was that she was very good at her job. In most branches of government, gender quotas were essential, although less so in those more secret areas. In their initial meeting, Natasha had expected an identikit discussion. But that hadn't happened either.

Amanda didn't talk about gender and she didn't talk about race either. In fact, she had made it clear that she didn't give a hoot about any of that and would do what she needed to get the job done. Amanda would be a better friend than an enemy, and Natasha already had confidence in her. Amanda was a maverick, and you had to be good to be a maverick in the corridors of power.

Although Natasha enjoyed the high-powered title of Head of HR, she was currently working in a poorly lit and worse-smelling basement. Some of the records had been haphazardly computerised a couple of years ago, but the project had been pursued casually, so the volume of physical storage continued to grow, home to a variety of top-secret documents as well as pretty much everything else that was three or more years old.

The storage was imperfectly arranged in boxes of varying size on crude and dusty metal racking, so Amanda's apparently simple demand to provide a list of all agents active in the last ten years was not guaranteed a speedy resolution.

The indexing of the archive was also part of a much-deferred project, so it was many hours before Natasha eventually located a file with a vague reference to a Robert Lennon. It was a start, but it wasn't much. The trouble with agencies like MI1 was that even the internal records, to the extent they were complete, were arranged with secrecy in mind. Records of operations may never have been kept, with so many operations requiring comprehensive deniability. In such circumstances, very often the best research method was to talk to long-serving staff. Gerard would be as good as anyone.

Her luck was improving; she found a thin, more formal, personnel file with the name Robert Lennon on the front. She was temporarily excited, but the contents were disappointing. All it contained was that Lennon had been a member of MI1 and his previous Glasgow address.

The fingerprints, dental and DNA records of all staff had been included in the computerised records. Lennon's full-service records continued to elude her, and she tutted and settled down for a long session.

Chapter 17

In Longtown police station, Emma Dixon sat behind her desk and reflected on her case over a morning coffee. It was her first murder. She had long wanted to lead a murder case, but this was a murder with a twist. She knew Lennon and she hadn't liked him, and she was going to have to question friends. No one said it was going to be easy.

She focused on professional matters. This was a chance for her to impress. Her career had proceeded reasonably satisfactorily so far, but, based in Longtown, scope for promotion was limited. She had been offered two chances to leave the area in the past year, but she had turned them both down. She wondered how many more chances she would get. Personal, rather than professional, considerations had blocked her then, and now she regretted those decisions.

Emma had been a police officer for ten years, but she had been married longer than that. Just eighteen and an infatuation with a local boy. It had been fine at first, but it soon became clear that she was the one with all the potential and ambition. As she grew, she had changed and he hadn't, and for several long years now, the marriage had become loveless and husband and wife contrived to encounter each other as little as possible. That was easier for her to contrive than he, as shift work and the demands of the police force disrupted most domestic lives.

Partial estrangement was just about manageable for her, but recently he had come to resent it and become increasingly insecure. When he realised that he might lose her, he sought to control her. It was intolerable, and, as recently as this morning, Emma stood accused of sleeping with everyone in the police force and most men in the town.

That was a laugh. She was nearly thirty and she had only ever slept with him. She used to believe in loving, honouring and, maybe, even obeying, but no longer. He had had so many chances, but she knew now that unless she made a change, violence was inevitable. She cursed herself when, in an unaccountable moment, she felt sorry for men. They were the weaker sex. They never knew when they had lost a woman's love. As for her, in the last few months she had started to notice men. At first it had been strange and she felt it was wrong, but no longer.

She thought about Jack Edwards. He was well off, apparently single and was fun to be with. She thought that maybe he liked her, but probably not. He was an interesting man, but miles too old for her. His relationship with Amanda Barratt seemed to go beyond professional. At the very least, she seemed to trust him completely. When they had met, Amanda had been professional and had joked a bit about Jack, but Emma was a detective as well, and she sensed there was more.

She had thought enough about Jack Edwards, so she refocused onto her case. A forensic report lay before her and she re-read it carefully. It was disappointingly short of detail and merely confirmed what she already knew. The gun had not been recovered, but it was probably a Browning – standard issue for many branches of the British armed forces up until a decade or so ago. Lennon had worked at the airbase and he had a gun. Val Fraser had confirmed this, but the gun was missing.

At least a hundred locals still resident in the town had worked at the airbase, but in Emma's favour, only a smaller group had been issued with side-arms. Further in her favour, only a smaller subset

– maybe twenty or so – had been legally allowed to retain their weapons after the base had closed. A list would have been a help, but compiling one was already proving a challenge. The trouble was that this group consisted of operatives who, although nominally based at the airbase, were often controlled by the most covert groups of the British state, and many had been involved in the troubles in Northern Ireland, which was twenty miles away as the crow flew.

Emma decided to concentrate on what she *did* know. She knew people who hated Lennon and, despite what they had said earlier, she included Suzie and Peter Miller. Adam Jardine and Val Fraser could also not be excluded. Adam hadn't worked at the base, but he had been in the army, and as for Val, well, Emma hoped that she was in the clear. The intervention of Amanda Barratt was useful. She had already identified Lennon as a former military intelligence operative, and she was undeniably better placed to cut through any red tape at Whitehall.

However all this turned out, this was an important local case. Murder was rare in this part of the world. The area wasn't prosperous, but it was peaceful and the people were trusting. A speedy resolution was necessary. Otherwise, locals would eye each other differently and a little bit of what was good about the area would be lost. Emma wasn't going to have that on her watch.

Her deliberations were loudly interrupted by her desk phone. It wasn't good news.

She called in a constable. "Please go and get Mr Edwards at Canish and bring him to me. I'll be up at the Hillside Forest Trail. Meet me at the car park. You know it?"

He nodded and departed. Emma rose and, rounding up another constable, marched purposefully out of the station, wondering if murders really were like buses.

Chapter 18

About six miles south of Longtown, Emma and her colleague pulled into a layby alongside a police car. A uniformed police officer stood smoking and talking to a man with a fishing rod. He threw aside his cigarette. "Morning, ma'am."

Emma nodded to her colleagues and addressed the fisherman. "Hello, Neil."

The officer and the fisherman led Emma and her colleague along a woodland path, closely enclosed by mixed woodland. Birds and small animals carried on with their business and the strong sun overhead intermittently streamed through the woodland canopy. A walk of a few hundred yards took them beyond the copse, and all followed an indistinct path round a small lochan until they reached a small wooden hut. She took a step back.

"The door is unlocked, ma'am"

She stood in front of the door, took a deep breath and pushed it open. It gave easily. The shed was small, maybe ten feet square. Inside was neatly arranged: a bed, and an extensive but tidily arranged collection of fishing, camping and cooking gear. It was also home to a fair amount of wildlife, mostly the solid black cloud of flies and bluebottles that buzzed over the body of what looked like a man. Emma took a step backwards and shut her eyes involuntarily as the shed ejected a cloud of insects.

She turned to the fisherman. "You found this, Neil?"

"Yes."

"What time?"

"Well, I was up at the big lochan over the hill first thing this morning. I spent a couple of hours there, but there was nothing doing so I came down here about ten, I think."

"Alone?"

"Yes."

"Was the shed door shut when you got down here?

"As far as I could see, yes."

"Why did you go into the shed?" she asked.

"I thought it might have a few fishing flies or something."

"When was that?"

"About ten minutes after I arrived, ten past ten, maybe quarter past."

"Did you touch the body?"

The fisherman grimaced. "Fuck no."

"Do you know him?"

The fisherman peered inside. "Well, I haven't had a good look at his face, but I do know that a man called Brannigan owns this shed. I've never met him, but I've heard he's a bit of an oddball, a sort of ageing hippy, no fixed address."

Emma looked at the policeman, who shook his head. "Don't know him, ma'am. As for the times, that sounds about right. I got a call from Neil about ten-thirty, and I was coming back from Glasgow."

"Why didn't you call 999?" Emma asked.

The fisherman said, indicating the policeman, "Tom lives next door. He's the police."

Emma half shrugged and half nodded. It was how things worked here. "Did you see anyone at all this morning?"

"Not a soul."

"Okay, get a full statement. Thanks, Neil."

The fisherman said, "Am I okay to go afterwards?"

"Yes, but not a word about this to anyone in town."

He nodded unconvincingly.

"Tom," Emma said, "see if you can find out anything about this Brannigan and let me know."

Constable Tom nodded, and he and the fisherman departed, leaving Emma and her colleague in sole possession of the scene. "Phone Glasgow. Get the forensic team back here."

The constable walked around to optimise his phone signal, and Emma gingerly returned to the shed. The swarm of flies had thinned a little, but the comparative silence was replaced by the smell: rancid and sickly in the sweltering heat of the shed. Lennon's body hadn't smelled like this yesterday. Brannigan, if that was who it was, had died before him.

A voice behind said, "Hello."

She turned with a start. Jack Edwards stood alongside her and pushed his head into the shed to share the view. He wasn't in there long. "Jeez, nasty. Has he been dead a while?"

"More than a day, at least two, I would say."

"Who is he?"

"Might be the guy that owns the shed, name of Brannigan, but we don't know that yet. It seems the shed was always unlocked, so it could be anyone."

Emma repressed another retch.

Jack looked at her intently and she shifted uncomfortably. Amanda Barratt wouldn't retch, she was sure.

Her phone broke the silence.

"We're in luck." she said, after hanging up. "The forensic team are still in town. They'll be here in fifteen minutes."

Emma led Jack away from the hut. She sat on some rocky ground and he alongside. He lit a cigarette and offered her one. She hesitated but declined, so they waited in silence until a team of four plain-clothed individuals arrived and got straight to work.

The day was fine and, in other circumstances, it would have been a grand spot to enjoy the countryside and the panoramic sea views. But all Emma could think of was the tiny white screen wrapped tightly around the shed.

"Did you have a close look around in there?" Jack asked.

Emma grimaced. "Close enough."

"Definitely murder?"

"Looks like it. There's a fair amount of blood around his neck"

Jack speculated idly. "I wonder if he was killed in the shed or put there?"

"No idea."

"Do you think this has got anything to do with Lennon's death?"

"We've had two murders in the last twenty years," Emma said. "Now two in two days?"

"Quite a coincidence," Jack agreed.

"Still, there's no obvious connection at this stage."

Emma stood up as a familiar face approached. "This is Doctor Wilson," she said to Jack.

Wilson took off a glove, inspected his hand and, satisfied, extended it.

"Jack Edwards, Home Office."

"Home Office, hmmm?" Wilson said. He turned to Emma. "Well, it'll be a while before we finish, but you'll want some preliminary details."

"If you can."

Wilson was a man of few words. "Male, mid-forties and dead at least two days. Cause of death, massive loss of blood, probably, from a wound on the neck, near the main artery. Death would have been nearly instantaneous."

"Was he killed in the shed?" Emma asked.

Wilson considered. "I don't think so. Distribution of the blood tells against that. Besides, I think there's blood outside the shed, but that'll take a day or so to confirm."

"No chance of a weapon?"

"Sorry, Emma."

"And what would I be looking for?"

Wilson shook his head. "Ordinary knife maybe, but really too early to tell." He turned his head and conducted a panoramic review. "If it were me and I had a knife, well, I would take it with me. If I had to get rid of it, maybe the peatbogs, lochans, or maybe I'd just walk up the hill and chuck it into the Irish Sea."

Emma said, "So, if he's murdered, how did the murderer get here? Walk or . . ." She stroked her chin. "Drive?"

Jack shrugged. "What about footprints around the hut?"

"We've had about four consecutive dry days," Wilson said. "We can check but I doubt we'll get anything."

"Can you check the car park?"

He nodded. "Yes, I'll do that. Now, unless there's anything else, I've got to get on." He added dryly, "Maybe I need to open an office down here, Emma?"

"Maybe," she conceded sadly.

Wilson left and got back to work, and Emma took out her phone and commissioned reinforcements for a search of the area. "Brannigan: do you know that name?" This enquiry elicited a long response and Emma spent a long time listening, contributing only a couple of grunts. She eventually ended the call and tilted her head back.

Jack looked at her expectantly.

She turned to him. "Seems like the man in the shed is another one of Amanda's pensioners."

Chapter 19

Amanda was impressed. Natasha Gold hadn't got everything, but she had done well. She had confirmed Lennon as an asset of MI1 – last active about half a dozen years ago. He had been part of a surveillance unit and been engaged in various operations about which she had no information at present.

Lennon's death would probably be of no interest to her and her directorate. Local evidence suggested he had plenty of enemies. Retired MI1 agents had a right to be privately murdered just like everybody else.

She wondered how Jack was getting on. Enjoying himself, most likely. Jack would be enjoying working with Emma Dixon. She sighed. Men were such fools. Forever in their late teens . . . men just never knew when they were beaten. Emma Dixon was too young for Jack, and she was too steady for him. He would find this out soon.

Amanda liked Jack, and she wasn't too young for him.

The telephone interrupted these idle musings. She was momentarily resentful, but the call proved to be interesting.

She got up and left her office. There was only a lone computer operator in the open-plan area. Amanda hadn't been properly introduced. Now was as good a time as any. Extending a hand, she said, "I'm Amanda Barratt, the new director. Could you find

Natasha Gold for me? I think she's in the basement, in the records department, and I've no idea where that is."

The computer operator accepted her hand and scuttled off.

A moment later, Natasha Gold was back in Amanda's office.

"I've got another name for you," Amanda said. "Patrick Brannigan. It seems we may have lost another of our pensioners."

Natasha Gold had better news this time. "I've seen that name. Just give me a minute." Without further explanation she jogged out of the office and returned a few minutes later. She handed Amanda a single sheet.

"Natasha," Amanda said as she read, "what are the odds of two of our former assets being found dead in a remote part of Scotland in the last three days?"

"Long."

"This exercise just got a bit more important. We've got two guys, with us at the same time, and probably doing the same kind of work. I want everything you can get on them. Did they know each other? What work? What cases did they work on? Who controlled them? I want everything."

Natasha nodded and opened her mouth as if to say something then clamped it shut. Amanda regarded her curiously. What had she been about to say? And where on earth was Gerard Gaines?

Chapter 20

Amanda decided not to wait for the results of Natasha's further researches. She made a call and pulled in a favour. Within half an hour she was sitting in a club in Whitehall opposite her nominal boss.

Tony Cuthbert was a politician and the current defence minister of the United Kingdom. Neither of them would have sat here fifty years ago. He was a working-class boy who had made it, and she was a woman. Still, here they were, and she appraised him as he ordered some coffee. He was about forty and well dressed. Confidence emanated from him, but was it genuine? He had no obvious qualifications for his current job. He was an accountant by trade. Despite that, he was popularly considered left wing, already a veteran of many activist causes.

Amanda didn't like activists and she didn't like Cuthbert. It was a bad start, although he didn't appear to reciprocate her enmity. He poured coffee and said, "Very nice to meet you, Miss Barratt. I have heard many good things about you."

She accepted these anonymous testimonials easily. "Good to meet you, Minister."

Cuthbert was theoretically Amanda's boss, but he had more of a non-executive role. "What can I do for you?"

"Well, I thought, of course, I would take this opportunity to introduce myself, but I do have a small query."

Cuthbert waited.

"You have been defence minister for about eighteen months."

He corrected her. "Two years."

She apologised. "I am checking out a couple of things at the moment, specifically concerning surveillance operations. Have you authorised any in the last two years through MI1?"

He thought for only a few seconds. "No, nothing at all." He added, realistically, "Not that I am aware of every security operation."

That was fair enough and Amanda believed him. She knew Cuthbert was not her key interviewee and brought the encounter to an abrupt end.

She regained the streets of London and pulled out her mobile. A short conversation ensued and her luck was in. Her real boss was also in Whitehall, and it proved just as easy for her to get an audience.

Nick Devoy was a working-class boy also, but he wore it easily and had never changed. Amanda had known him for many years but had never worked for him. He was about fifty and dressed more casually than the public might have expected from one of Britain's top spies. Devoy hadn't directly appointed her, but he would have been consulted. Nominally they both ran a directorate, but there was a difference between her twenty-strong unit and his thousands of specialists in Cheltenham. It was understood that, by convention, MI1 reported to Cheltenham as well as the minister.

"Hello, Nick."

He smiled. "You want coffee?"

"No, I just had some with Tony Cuthbert."

"Ah, you have met our minister? How was he?"

"Okay, it was a very short meeting."

Devoy nodded. "Cuthbert's all right - for a politician. Quite easy to deal with."

This was the normal criterion by which ministers tended to be judged, and Amanda nodded.

"I'm surprised to see you," Devoy added. "Haven't you just started?"

"Yes, first week, in fact," Amanda said, "but something came up."

Devoy sympathised with a shrug.

"I have got a couple of dead bodies. Two surveillance operative assets from about ten years ago. Names of Lennon and Brannigan."

Devoy shook his head.

"Yes, I didn't think you would know them, but what I really want to know is how these surveillance teams operated."

Devoy nodded. "Well, they were only set up about ten years ago and they operated for a short time, just four or five years. They were ultra-secret targeted surveillance exercises. Then they were replaced with satellites and that sort of thing."

"Who did they target?" Amanda asked.

"High-profile targets. Blanket twenty-four-hour surveillance. The best person to speak to would be David Preece. Do you know him?"

"Ex-defence minister?"

"Yes."

"Where is he now?" Amanda asked.

"Not sure. I think he went to the City. Retired from politics."

"Should be easy to find."

Devoy agreed. Then he added something interesting. "I think these units were generally three-men teams."

Amanda exhaled. "Great, our records are already struggling with the two names we have at the moment."

Devoy sympathised. "I doubt that there'll be records of some of this anyway."

"Will Preece know much?"

Devoy scoffed. "Of course not. He was the minister for some of their operational time, and I think it was him who disbanded them. But a minister would never know the operators, just Control.

But if you need details, then surely the answer's in your own directorate?"

She looked quizzically at Devoy.

"These units were handled by Gerard Gaines."

Chapter 21

A black cab screeched to a halt and the driver cursed out of the cab window. Gerard Gaines barely heard him. He walked on and reached the other side of the road unscathed. His head was spinning. The meeting with Preece hadn't helped. Preece had been as confident as ever but Gaines wasn't. He owed very nearly a million pounds to people who could best be described as unauthorised, and they wanted it back now.

An oncoming pedestrian scolded him on his pavement manners and Gaines raised his head with a start. He was outside a Tube station. He entered and, without conscious decision, found himself on a crowded train. On auto-pilot he got off at Paddington and within half an hour he was at Cookham.

He strode robotically out of the station, ignored the single taxi on the rank and walked towards the town centre. He managed about a quarter of a mile past a classic car garage and the Stanley Spencer museum. Spencer painted startling oils of resurrections, but Gaines didn't fancy his own chances. He looked up and spied a taxi. He hailed it and spared his exhausted body the last mile over the river and then along its bank.

Most of the houses that sat alongside the Thames were valued in millions, but not Gaines' single-bedroomed cottage. In the old days it had been the gardener's digs on an estate that comprised many acres, but the house and ancestral lands had been sold and most of the money had gone to Gaines' ex-wife. Admittedly, he had squandered about a million pounds mostly on things he couldn't really remember. He walked to the end of a private lane and took the few steps to the front door of the cottage. He retrieved his house key from an overhanging plant pot, dipped his head to enter and went straight to the cabinet, where he poured himself a large whisky. He flopped into a seat and stared into space, exhausted and feverishly trying to rationalise a coherent plan and quieten the screaming voices in his head.

Chapter 22

In central London, Natasha was irritated but not yet concerned by the fact that Gerard Gaines had not returned to the office. She had waded through countless boxes of records, but still didn't have all she wanted. Given the state of the records this wasn't unsurprising, but she was still disappointed. She wanted to surprise and impress Amanda. There was still a chance to do that, but she needed to speak to Gerard. She replaced a pile of unsorted records back into a box and left it on the wooden table. Sounds from above encouraged her to take a break from the dismal basement, but upstairs the main office was empty, only broken by the sound of papers shuffling. She turned and followed the sound.

Julian Johns sat behind Amanda's desk.

"Hi, Julian."

He looked up and nodded.

"Amanda not back?"

"No, I have no idea where she is," Johns said. "Anything I can do?"

Natasha liked Julian, even though they never agreed on anything. Some viewed them as rivals, but both of them understood that there was enough room in the British security services for a couple of high-flyers, so they worked well together.

Natasha flopped onto an armchair. "Oh, she's asked me about a couple of dead guys. Used to work here."

Johns continued leafing through a thick report, making utterances and annotations on the pages.

"Something to do with a couple of ex-assets, names of Lennon and Brannigan. They worked for us about ten years ago. Surveillance guys."

Johns looked up and then back at the report. "Bit before my time." He looked across at her. "I think I've heard about these units, but surely they've been shut down for years?"

Natasha nodded. "Yes, I can't find a thing downstairs."

"You want a hand?"

Natasha sighed. "Thanks, but I'm okay. I'll go through the basement again. I've probably missed something. Besides," she added, "you must be busy today. I thought you were on holiday?"

"Yes, tomorrow for a couple of days. I want to get the report finished before I go."

"Going somewhere nice?"

"No, nothing planned. I'll be back next week."

She rose. "Have a good time."

She moved back towards the stairs to the basement but then stopped and turned. Gerard was probably home now. He would be more help with her enquiries, and she was sick of the basement. She picked up her coat and left Julian Johns to his report.

Chapter 23

When there was something wrong, there was only one place that Gerard liked to go. Natasha quickly hailed a taxi outside the office and within fifteen minutes she was on the Cookham train. It was delayed five or so minutes, which annoyed her, as did the absence of taxis at the country station. She didn't wait. It was a walk of about a mile through the village and then over the river to the north.

She turned off the main road and onto the start of an expensive private road network. Behind the gates and high walls, large family homes gradually grew into mansions until she arrived at Gerard's small cottage. All was calm, and birdsong now overwhelmed the distant sound of traffic. She passed over the few paving stones and knocked hard on the door. Nothing happened. She reached up to the plant pot, but it was empty. This was probably a good sign. She knocked again, three times. Her knuckles hurt. Her heart was racing and then from inside came sounds of hope. The indistinct sound gathered into the discernible sound of someone approaching the door. Her heart raced as the oak door opened slowly, very slowly. Gerard looked worn and haggard, but that didn't matter for the moment, and she, overwhelmed, with relief, enveloped him in her arms.

That he was in a bad way was obvious, and they stumbled together into the house and sat beside each other on a sofa. He said nothing and seemed incapable of speech. She just wanted to hold him.

They sat together for a long time until, at last, he broke the silence. He looked up and flicked his greying hair off his face. "I'm so sorry."

Natasha wasn't yet sure what he was sorry for, but she wasn't going to force the issue. She broke her hold and went through to the small kitchenette. There wasn't much, but there was a jar of mediocre instant coffee and she made two mugs. She gave him one and this time sat in the chair opposite.

He said, in a low faltering voice, "I love you, Natasha."

"I know, Gerard. I love you too. Whatever it is, **we** can sort it."

He laughed mirthlessly. "I doubt it, Tasha, I really doubt it."

"Is it a long story, Gerard?"

"Yes, sorry, it is."

She was working hard to keep the anxiety from her features. "Let's hear it."

On the second telling, Natasha was in bad shape too. He was alive, but beyond that, his prospects were indeed desperate. She doubted that he believed her repeated entreaties that there was a way out of this. She wasn't sure whether she believed them either, but she was going to try. A germ of an idea was forming in her mind. It could work, but it would depend on Gerard staying strong.

She wondered whether he had enough strength left. He looked a bit better now, but he was exhausted after his confession and sat endlessly smoking in silence.

Natasha's mind was racing and her head was throbbing, but as she looked at Gerard, she knew that she was going to have to do the thinking for both of them. She said firmly, "As for the money, this house can go. If we sell the London house too, we can raise the full amount."

"And where will we live?"

"We'll work on that later, let's just see if we can work out some kind of plan. As to the rest, we can't deny involvement, but you can say you didn't know the status of the units. Blame David Preece."

"No, no, there are records of payments. Besides, I was Control."

Natasha changed tack. "Well, there are no records of the operations."

He managed a low laugh. "Obviously not."

"So, unless Preece talks, why would this come out?"

Gaines looked at her. "It's not so simple, Natasha. The skipper's been killed."

Natasha narrowed her eyes. "Who's the skipper?"

"Lennon, Bobby Lennon."

Natasha uttered a groan that she tried but was too late to suppress.

Gaines said sharply, "You knew that?"

She couldn't avoid the question. "Well, I have heard the name. In fact, Amanda Barratt asked about him today. I was looking for his records most of yesterday."

Gaines groaned now too. "Did you find anything?"

"Not much."

A clock on the mantelpiece ticked deafeningly through the silence. She said, "Do you know a man called Brannigan?"

Gaines shook his head wearily. "Who's that?"

"Oh, just another name Amanda Barratt asked about. Maybe it's nothing to do with anything. Although ..."

"Although what?"

"Although he was killed in the same area, Longtown in Scotland."

Gerard looked desperate, and she needed to shut this thread down. "Look, never mind that. As far as I can see, these illegal operations are not known yet and I don't see why they should come out. Let's concentrate on the money side for now."

She got up and went across to a sideboard groaning with bottles. She filled two large tumblers and sat down close beside him. She nudged him until he turned his face to hers and looked at him hard. He had perked up a bit. "We will get through this."

They drank in silence with their own thoughts and their hands locked tightly together. For a moment, in their bubble, all was calm, but the moment didn't last. It was only a low knock on the front door but it felt like an erupting volcano. Natasha jumped to her feet.

Surprisingly, Gerard was on his feet before her. He looked partially restored. "I'll go – it'll be a neighbour. I'll get rid of them."

He walked purposely to the door and then disappeared from view. She heard the door open and Gerard, still in a steady voice, say, "Hello."

Nothing came back for a second and then an explosion, this time a real explosion, did all the talking.

It seemed like ages, but she was up and beside him in seconds.

Gerard's face was intact, even peaceful, but most of his torso was ripped open and disarranged. She didn't scream and she didn't stop to worry that the killer might still be outside. Blindly, she ran onto the road and, in an instant, decided to turn right and back towards the village.

The road started straight but turned after a few hundred yards. Her heart thumped and her lungs felt as if they were bursting, but today she had wings, and with long frantic strides and endless stamina, she gained the corner. There was a reward for her energy. It wasn't first prize, but it was something. Just a glimpse. A figure getting into a car and speeding onto the main public road. She was young and she had young eyes, and this was all she needed. Further pursuit was now impossible, and, consumed with rage, she retraced her steps to the cottage, contemplating how she would respond to the end of her world.

Chapter 24

Jack dialled the Longtown police station. "Is that Emma? I mean, DI Dixon?"

"Hello, Jack." It sounded like she was smiling.

"I've had a call with Amanda, and she's given me a bit of an update."

"Oh good, I spoke to her yesterday but all she said was that Patrick Brannigan was another of hers."

"Anything happening your end?"

"No, in fact, I was just wondering about the next steps. Really, I need to wait on the forensic team's report on Brannigan."

"Yeah, anyway, you want me to come over?"

"No, I'll come over to you, get out of the office. I'll see you in ten minutes."

Jack looked around the villa and wondered how he could improve it before her arrival. Fortunately, he hadn't been here long enough to make a mess, so his duties were light. He emptied two full ashtrays and removed a used plate from the far end of the sofa. The cool of the early evening restricted the amount of natural air he could stand admitting from outside, and he settled for three long squirts from an air freshener.

She arrived in ten minutes and accepted coffee.

Jack didn't really have all that much new information. How could he string it out? He wanted some company and he wanted to talk to her, not necessarily about business. He was in luck. She sank deeply into a chair and let out a long sigh.

"Tough day?" he asked.

"Not really. Nothing much has happened since you left."

"Did you go home?"

She smiled and shook her head. It was a smile that Jack recognised. He was right.

"God knows I wish I could, but, well, there's not much fun at home these days," she said.

It was a minor invitation to proceed and he accepted it. "Er, what about your husband?" he asked clumsily.

She laughed sadly and slowly shook her head.

Jack was interested but not nosy. "Sorry, none of my business."

She laughed again and said pleasantly, "No, don't worry. Everyone knows. It's like that in Longtown." She paused. "I've been married for about ten years but, well, we've kind of grown apart."

As she spoke her expression hardened. There was a suspicion of a tear in her eye, but he couldn't tell whether it was anger or sadness.

Jack looked at her. He liked her. A wild thought that she would leap into his arms entertained him for a minute, but it didn't happen. This was probably a good thing. He wasn't much of a seducer.

She quickly recovered most of her lost composure and sat up straighter in the chair. She crossed her legs and become DI Dixon again. In her professional voice she said, "So you have spoken to Amanda. What did she say?"

Jack recounted the details of the brief conversation, essentially advising that Amanda was making some more in-depth enquiries at her end and would call both of them tomorrow.

Quite obviously this information could have been conveyed over the phone, so he added, "Perhaps local and more detailed enquiries can wait until after the call."

Amanda had said no such thing, but it seemed implied.

Emma said, "Yes, we are trying to get all the forensic and crime scene stuff finalised today and then we'll take it from there. Who is Amanda talking to in London?"

"Not sure, to be honest. Government people, I think."

Emma shrugged. "Well, she can update us tomorrow." She had finished her drink.

"You want a refill?"

She accepted the fresh drink, relaxed back in her chair, and started on a new line of questions. "Tell me about Amanda."

He wasn't sure how much information she was after, so he responded with the minimum. "She's under forty, which I think is important to her, although she doesn't admit it."

Emma laughed.

"She's had a number of successful careers. As an academic, then a policewoman. I think she was a Commander in the Met for a while and then, I think, Special Branch. I can never keep up. Now, well, I'm not sure how to describe her job. A spy, probably."

Emma had apparently learnt enough about Amanda's curriculum vitae. "Married?"

"Divorced," Jack replied. "She did pretty well out of it. Her husband was very wealthy." Jack was pretty sure money was of importance to women but Emma just looked at him sharply.

"So how do you know her?"

"Well, at one time she was an academic editor – years ago – that's when I first met her."

"You were an academic?" she said, raising an eyebrow.

"Yes, at one time."

"In what field?"

"History and a bit of economics."

She nodded vaguely, seemingly unimpressed. "Do you still do it?"

"No, I gave it up about three or four years ago."

"And worked for Amanda since?"

He laughed. "No, no. I don't work for Amanda."

She looked slightly alarmed.

He reassured her. "Sorry, I mean, I do work with her from time to time. Don't worry, I have signed the Official Secrets Act and all that, and I'm licensed to carry these things." He indicated the two Glocks on the occasional table.

Her expression relaxed. "So just some part-time work?"

He nodded.

Emma cheered him up then. "Surely you are a bit young to be semi-retired? Are Amanda's engagements very lucrative?"

It was a bit nosy of her, but he wanted her to be nosy about him.

"No, they're not. In fact, I don't get paid." He suppressed an urge to boast about his wealth.

"So how do you manage?" she asked. "I mean the hotel conversion."

He laughed. "There are drawbacks in having a small family, but some advantages if you are the only nephew of a very wealthy maiden aunt."

Emma's expression flickered. Wealthy was a relative term. She looked tempted to ask how much he was worth, but just asked, "Are you married, Jack?"

Jack experienced a short, sharp melancholic shock when he thought about Marion. "No. I was with someone but, well, she died. That was a few years ago."

"Sorry, clumsy of me."

Jack flashed a reassuring smile. "No, it's okay. Not your fault. It feels a long time ago."

But this proved a conversation stopper, so Jack rose and poured himself a whisky. "You want one?"

She declined this time and began to study her mobile. She sent a text and received one back.

A few minutes later there was a knock at the door and the young constable who Jack had met earlier took her away.

Chapter 25

David Preece was having another easy day. Yesterday, he had reassured Gaines a little and he had heard nothing. Hopefully Gaines had calmed down. He was about to meet Amanda Barratt, who he had vaguely heard of, but that didn't matter. The meeting would be straightforward and routine. In anticipation of her arrival he spread out a number of files on his desk. He rang through for a cup of coffee and then carelessly scanned the documents.

The bottom-line numbers were high and satisfactory, but much of the analysis was convoluted and abstruse, and Preece had long since given up pretending he understood it. He threw down the sheets and took a mouthful of coffee. The phone rang. Amanda Barratt was early. This was annoying. He could have kept her waiting, but that wasn't much of a gambit, so he exited his office and went into the reception area to welcome her.

Preece's initial impressions were favourable. She was a bit younger than him. She was slim and her jet-black hair, her powerful blue eyes and her perfect figure made a good package. He indicated a chair to her and she sat, and he did likewise.

"Nice to meet you, Miss Barratt. How can I help you?"

She accepted this invitation immediately. "I'm director of MI1 and I've got two dead former agents, Mr Preece. They worked for MI1 when you were the minister in charge. I wondered if you could tell me anything about them."

He leant back in his seat, and his face flushed a bit. "Well, I will do what I can, Miss Barratt, but that's about ten years ago."

"You were the responsible minister for four or five years I think?"

"Yes, about that. I moved to the Treasury after that."

"Yes, I know. However, I'm pretty new in this job and anything you can tell me will be a help. My enquiries are purely routine."

Preece sat forward a bit and presented her with a smile. He tilted his head and said, "Yes, I quite understand. Now let me think. There were only a few operations in my time. Can't even remember what they were." He spread his hands. "You know how it is – sign here, Minister, and, well, you just sign."

Amanda looked at him closely. "Bobby Lennon and Patrick Brannigan."

He made another gesture with his hands. "Who are they?"

"The dead agents, Mr Preece."

"Oh sorry, of course. Well, I've never heard of either of them."

"Well, no reason you should," Amanda said. "They were field guys. They worked in a covert operational listening squad."

Preece forced his face to stay blank.

"Who did you deal with at MI1?" she asked.

"Let me think. Well, various folks. The director at that time was Peter, Peter Springer. I think he's retired now."

"Yes, about five years ago. Gerard Gaines has been acting head since then. Do you know him, Mr Preece?" Amanda asked.

"Yes, I know Gerard. Haven't seen him recently, but he was often the point man. Nice chap. How is he doing?"

"Actually, I've not met him yet. These operational units were decommissioned by you?"

"Yes."

"Did you initiate this?"

"Again, not really," Preece said. "We, that is the new government, commissioned an efficiency report and, as I remember, this was part of the review recommendations."

"Who did you deal with over that?"

"I think it was Gerard. Really on my part it was just a signature. Gerard is the best man to ask."

"And there's nothing else you can tell me about these operations and the operatives?"

He shook his head. "No, nothing whatsoever. As I say, it was ten years ago."

"Thanks, Mr Preece," Amanda said. "It's likely that I'll need to talk to you again. This investigation is likely to be extensive. I mean, losing two of one's former agents in one's first week looks careless." She rose and shook his hand. "I'll see myself out. Thanks."

Preece made to get up but she was out the door before he could deliver his final platitudes. He walked back slowly to his desk, wondering what to make of the interview and Miss Barratt. He decided everything had gone well.

A ring from his desk phone cut short these assessments. He picked it up and listened. There was another door in his room and it connected to an adjoining office. Preece went through and, after attending a very short impromptu board meeting, was forced to concede that his analysis had been wrong.

Chapter 26

The assassin's car was out of sight before Natasha turned and walked slowly back to the cottage in a daze. Misery, rage and a thirst for some kind of revenge competed for dominance. By the time she returned to the front door she resolved to park the misery and the rage. They could wait; there was a lifetime for that.

She entered the house and went through to the sitting room without glancing down at her dead lover. She picked up her bag and her coat, located the house key and locked and left the cottage without a backward glance. With Gerard dead, there was now no reason not to involve Amanda. But not yet.

A scout's pace took her along the private road and to the main road. She looked left and right. This was no time for economy, and she secured a taxi and headed for central London. It would probably have been quicker by train, but she didn't want to see anyone. The driver tried a vaguely political statement about climate change but he gave up when it went unanswered.

She stretched out her arm and looked at her hand. It was rock steady. Her heartbeat had returned to the background, and she wasn't in a hurry any more. Coldly, she calculated what she was going to do. She had never killed anyone; they said all agents might have to do that. She hadn't really believed that, but she believed it now. She was ready.

As she was lost in these thoughts, the journey passed quickly. She started as the driver cursed loudly at a cyclist and saw they were in the heart of London. After a few further dangerous manoeuvres, he turned into the mews and over the cobbles towards the home that she used to share with Gerard.

"Wait here," she said in a commanding voice that she barely recognised. "I'll be fifteen minutes. I need to go to the City. I'll pay you now."

She pushed five twenty-pound notes into his hand, which seemed to be satisfactory, and the driver nodded, lit a cigarette and reached for a tabloid newspaper.

She went inside and straight up the stairs. She felt very dirty, and tore her clothes off and into the walk-in shower.

Her hair was short and a quick brush was all it needed. Neither heels nor well-fitting designer clothes suited her purpose, so she settled for jeans, a white T-shirt and a leather jacket with many pockets. She descended the stairs and to the kitchen cupboard. It had been some time since her basic training, but she checked the Glock carefully and put it and three clips inside her jacket pocket.

In the drawer of the dresser there was a fair amount of cash and she pocketed it, along with a couple of bank and credit cards. She was ready. She locked the front door deliberately and got into the taxi.

The driver threw aside his newspaper. "Where to?"

She gave him an address. "I want you to drop me near this address but not on this street. Around the corner or something."

He nodded and smiled, unfazed by the request. He had heard everything before.

Getting from the mews house to the City took about as long as the journey from Cookham, giving her a chance to change her destiny, but her resolve never wavered. The taxi driver pulled up in a residential street. "Your address is just around the corner." He asked for no more money and sped away.

She walked a few steps until she stood at the end of Shore Street. It was a long road, consisting of endless mid-range terraced houses which were home to the working classes fifty years ago, but were now out of their price range.

Cars were parked on both sides of the street but the street was free of people.

This suited her and she began to walk. She didn't have heels and her steps were silent, but they boomed in her head until they were overwhelmed by her rising heartbeat. Outside Number 202, the car she knew she had seen earlier was there. She put her hand on the bonnet. The feedback was mixed, but the registration number was conclusive.

For a second, she considered a casual front-door assault. It had worked well for the assassin. She rejected this approach and continued to walk past the house. She would wait. A few hundred yards on was a small children's park. She entered it and, after rejecting a bench, selected a swing to sit upon. When moved forward a little, it allowed for an uninterrupted view of the front door of Number 202. She waited.

Chapter 27

As she pushed the swing gently to and fro, Natasha, for the first time since she had left the cottage, thought of Gerard. He was always likely to die before her and she had thought she was prepared for that. But not like this.

She wondered about him. He had been with her two hours ago, but where was he now? It was a big question. She hoped for the best and then chided herself. It was usual that folks turned to religion in times of trauma, but she was a modern woman who had no need of superstition. But at times like this, maybe everyone, even her, needed something bigger to believe in.

She continued to mentally wrestle with the proposition of the existence of a supreme being and, to her annoyance, could think of nothing beyond the usual superficial arguments. If God existed, why did he let such things happen? There was no answer to this. Had Gerard been such a bad person? Was it fair?

She thought about the story he had told her last night. Certainly, there was a clear case that much of it was wrong, but still, Gerard, her man, didn't deserve death. She was sure of that. It was time for a bit of self-reproach and she obliged herself. In retrospect, it was clear that he had changed very much over the last months. She had noticed but had simply assumed that it had been nothing more than the natural ups and downs of a modern age.

Well, it had been more than that, and she had missed it or ignored it. And for that she had lost him.

She decided to abandon these reflections and re-focus herself on her immediate task. There was a short break through the clouds of revenge and hate and it allowed for a short period of calmer assessment. She was no killer. She had no experience of this sort of thing. But one had to start somewhere, and the slaying of a lover's killer seemed the right place. There remained the practical details. Clearly, her target had more experience than she did. He had a kill count of at least one, probably more.

Up until about four hours ago, she had quite liked Julian Johns. Although, as she reflected, she realised she knew almost nothing about him. She had always thought they were similar types, loners and outsiders. They were both devoted to work and openly ambitious. She wondered why Johns had never come on to her. Maybe women weren't his thing, or was it all people? She had never heard him talking of friends.

She expelled a thought of pity for Johns and returned to the proposed venture. She still had enough rage in her head, but it was now accompanied by a sprinkling of logic. Logic broke through. With Gerard dead, there was now no reason that the story should be suppressed.

She wavered for the first time. She had a simple alternative. Phone Amanda and get this handled swiftly and professionally. She stared at her mobile. She was a professional, and she knew how to use a mobile phone. Only resolve eluded her, and it seemed impossible to summon it. She just couldn't direct her fingers to the phone. Rage and revenge couldn't be cast out, and they returned with a simple and overpowering plan: get up, go to the house, knock on the door and kill him.

This was simple and it made sense, so she pocketed her mobile and fingered the cold Glock. There was no one in the park and there was no one in the street. She looked for the safety on the gun, but these models didn't have a safety. The house was only about two hundred yards away. That was about twenty seconds away, if you were an Olympian runner. She wasn't, so, her features set hard and her eyes locked straight ahead, she settled for a brisk walking pace.

Now she had her hand on the gun and the house was no more than twenty yards away. Her mental rehearsals repeated in her brain. Her heart was thumping. Her resolution was unbroken, and she quickened her pace. She would do it.

As this final decision was taken, the game suddenly changed. Johns burst out of his house, slamming the front door behind him to a crashing close. He didn't look right or left, but unlocked his car and, without regard to anything other than his current objective, skilfully pulled the car out of its space and powered it down the road. At the park he turned left, and then Johns and his car were out of sight.

She stood fast for what seemed like a long time and then, with surprising difficulty, lowered herself onto a long low wall. It was a bit wet, but that hardly mattered.

Now she had no thoughts whatsoever, and she began to cry for her dead lover. It was wet overhead now, but that didn't matter. At last, she took her hand off her handgun and grasped her mobile. It was the first time she had phoned her boss, so hers was an unknown number. She wondered if Amanda would answer.

She did, and after Natasha stumbled through a few opening words, she sounded as if she had time to listen. Natasha stumbled through her story. To some, it would have sounded fantastic, but Amanda, with short punctuating words of encouragement, sounded as if she had heard such tales every day. She asked only two questions: the address of the cottage in Cookham and the car Johns was driving. Beyond this she made no comment until Natasha was too exhausted to talk on.

"Wait on the main Stretford Road," Amanda said. "I'll be there in fifteen minutes."

Shore Road was only a couple of streets behind the main drag, and Natasha got off the wet wall and began a slow amble to the rendezvous point. It wasn't a long walk but it took her a long time before the sudden roar of heavy traffic told her she was there.

With her head bowed, she passed people and shops before stopping outside a small independent car sales showroom. It had a decent amount of forecourt and a wide range of cars, all of which were on offer at, apparently, very competitive prices.

One glance at a two-year-old German saloon was all it took. A man was alongside. He was about twenty and was wearing a car salesman's uniform.

"Good choice," he said. "That's our car of the week. Less than ten thousand miles." He waved a set of keys at her. "How about taking her out?"

She wondered how he knew the car was female but didn't ask. He shook the keys again. She had nothing better to do, and although a new car was the last thing on her mind, she found herself nodding in response.

He opened the door with a flourish, handed her the keys, and directed her to the driver's seat. The door clicked shut and he moved round to the passenger door.

And then she had an idea. She knew these cars, and she knew all the buttons. The first button locked the doors and the second started the engine. Her right foot moved the car forward. Metal crunched sickeningly as the vehicle straddled a low concrete rise, but the salesman was right: the car was in good condition. A moment later she was on the main road, and a short break in the traffic and some favourable traffic lights allowed her to put half a mile of road between the car of the week and the open-mouthed salesman.

Chapter 28

Amanda was more shocked than she had been careful to sound when listening to Natasha Gold's story. If true, these killings went straight to the heart of her new directorate. She looked forward to one of the shortest ever directorial tenures in British Intelligence history. There wasn't time to worry about that now. She had dispatched a squad to Cookham and awaited their report and, with difficulty, commissioned a car and driver. MI1, she had discovered, had no pool cars, and she had yet again had to pull in a favour in Whitehall. A second favour in her first week was a bad start.

The car was well served with communications and also by a driver who announced himself as George. He was the right side of forty, about six feet tall and powerfully built. He also worked for Nick Devoy. Whether he could be completely trusted she had no idea, but, at the moment, he seemed a better bet than Julian Johns or Natasha Gold.

Gold's story, while fantastic, did not offend against the facts she had uncovered so far. That didn't make it true, but it was in Gold's favour. The traffic was heavy and progress was slow.

"How long?" she asked.

"About five minutes, ma'am, unless you want the siren on."

At this stage, a gain of five minutes didn't seem important. Besides, she wanted a report from Cookham before talking to

Natasha. "Quick as you can, but no siren. Get back onto Cookham and tell them to check in."

Her mobile rang. She listened. Gaines was certainly dead, albeit formal identification had not yet been conducted. A shotgun at close range and evidence that at least one other had been in the house. There were no further forensics at this stage. House-to-house enquiries were in progress but, despite the proliferation of security cameras in the partially gated community, no CCTV recording of a suspicious vehicle had yet been identified.

Nothing there told against Gold, but outside the world of espionage, the more prosaic explanation was that Gold had killed her lover. That was where the local CID would start. She thought about calling back, but it was early and Amanda was still minded to give Gold the benefit of the doubt.

As she reflected, the car slowed. "Right, we're looking for Natasha Gold," she said. "Late twenties, five feet nine, slim, good-looking, black hair and blue eyes." The rendezvous point had been loosely arranged, and after a slow drive which covered about half the length of the main street, there was no sign of her.

"Go to Shore Road, let's see if she's still there."

Her driver turned off the main road and they slowly crawled the length of Shore Road. There was no one. They returned to the main road, but Natasha was still nowhere to be seen.

"We need to get out."

In the absence of an obvious parking spot, George pulled into a car showroom. Amanda got out and George crossed the road. Amanda began to walk the near side of the street, but she had only taken a few steps when a man emerged from a sales office.

Amanda was in luck. He said something about a car of the week, but Amanda wasn't listening. She was looking over his shoulder and into the showroom office. There was another man there and he was talking to a uniformed policeman.

Amanda flashed a warrant card at the salesman. "What are the police here for?"

"Some crazy woman. She was viewing a car and just drove away with it."

"What did she look like?"

Despite her felonious behaviour, the salesman was also prepared to give Natasha Gold the benefit of the doubt. "Nice-looking, dark hair, about my age."

He was still talking, but Amanda was already on her way inside. She flashed her card again. She obtained the details of the car and deputised the officer to record the details, assuring the garage owners that they would get satisfaction in due course.

She left and, with a deafening shout, summoned George. Her voice overcame the roar of the traffic, and he turned and jogged back to her. She gave him a summary of the position.

"Maybe we'd better fill up?" he said.

It seemed a good idea, and he moved the car alongside a single fuel pump. Amanda picked up the car radio and checked in the two car registration numbers.

They were re-checked. "Okay, ma'am, tracking now," came over the radio.

George was finished refuelling and now began to expertly fiddle with buttons on the car console.

"Right," he said, "Alpha is seven miles away, going north but very slowly – it's tied up in traffic. Maybe heading for the M1? Beta about four miles away, going north, also slowly." He turned to her. "What now?"

"That traffic's not going to ease for some time."

"Not at this time of day, ma'am."

She had another idea. "How far are we from the City?"

When traffic regulations didn't apply, it wasn't far. "At this time of day, five minutes tops, ma'am."

"Can we get someone else to track these cars for twenty minutes or so?"

"Yes."

"Okay, do it. Tell them not intercept unless Beta approaches Alpha. Do not let that happen. If they judge it likely, pick up both cars and keep them apart."

Chapter 29

There was never anywhere to park in the City, so George drove onto the pavement and Amanda jumped out. An old soldier at the door came forward to remonstrate, but George's warrant card did the trick.

Amanda went through the swing doors and approached a smartly dressed receptionist. She would have many well-rehearsed reasons for turning folks away. "I'm afraid Mr Preece is not in this afternoon."

Amanda thought it might be true. She was in a hurry so she went for the moon-shot. "Sir Hector Laing?"

The receptionist paused before deciding on which excuse to deploy, but Amanda moved things forward. She flashed her warrant card. "I'm Amanda Barratt and I'm a director in MI1. This is urgent. Phone through for Sir Hector. Now."

This did the trick. With a vague expression of disgust, the defeated receptionist picked up a phone. She uttered a few words in a low voice and replaced the phone with a bang. In icy tones she said, "Someone will be with you shortly, if you would like to take a seat."

Amanda didn't bother with the seat and took only a step back from the desk. She twice looked at her watch, but it took less than a minute for a more senior assistant to swagger down the broad staircase. He looked as though he might know a lot more excuses, but instead he welcomed her and led her up well-carpeted stairs and into a spacious empty boardroom. He promised to return immediately, and he kept that promise.

She had never met Sir Hector Laing, but she knew what he looked like. He had been one of the country's most successful global businessmen and sometime corporate raider. It went without saying that he knew every recent prime minister on first-name terms and his network was about as powerful as one could have in Britain.

Amanda was well connected too, but this was a risk.

If Sir Hector was upset at being so rudely interrupted, he didn't show it. He was over seventy now, she guessed, but he was tall and he didn't stoop. His hair was only half-greying and, all in all, he cut an impressive physical figure. He sat alongside her casually and shook her hand.

"You work for Nick Devoy, Miss Barratt. What can I do for you?"

Name dropping already was a good start. "I need to talk to David Preece urgently. I am investigating three murders and he is either involved or has information that may be vital."

He looked at her, his face impassive. He said nothing.

Amanda had probably overplayed her hand. All she had was Gold's story, but she viewed Natasha Gold's theft of a car from the high street as another point in her favour. Would Gold have called her up, blurted out a long story and then done a runner in this most public of ways? She knew what Gold was doing. If so, it was even understandable in the circumstances. Having a partner shot in front of your own eyes was likely to provoke a reaction. "All these killings are related to a surveillance unit which we believed was inactive. We now have information that suggests differently, and Mr Preece is a close associate of one of the dead men."

"A moment, Miss Barratt." Sir Hector went out of the door and she heard low voices. He returned. "Mr Preece is on annual leave for a couple of days."

"Where is he?"

Sir Hector said breezily, "I'm afraid I have no idea. I can, of course, give you his private address. On a confidential basis, of course. Providing it is really necessary?"

Potential involvement in three murders seemed a good enough reason, but she let this go. "I already have his address. Why did you hire Preece?"

Sir Hector shrugged and said simply, "He is a decent front man and his political background means he has a lot of high-level connections."

That seemed fair qualifications for a salesman of an international hedge fund. She decided to push Laing a bit further. "I've heard a suggestion that Mr Preece was still involved with surveillance operations."

Sir Hector turned and looked at her. He looked surprised and demurred. "Hardly, he's been out of government for years – five or six, I think."

She held his gaze but it was difficult. His face was impassive. He withheld the pressure, and it was obvious that he had nothing else to say. The interview had come to a natural end. He walked towards the door. "I really don't know anything about these things. Obviously, you'll want to talk to David and, of course, I'm always happy to help."

Amanda accepted his invitation to leave and thanked him for his time without adding an unnecessary lie about being sorry to have troubled him. She hadn't got much, but she had marked his card. Whether he cared or was discomfited was not certain.

By the time she had returned to her badly parked car, George had bad news for her. "Preece is not at home. Should they wait on him?"

"Yes, find him and hold him. Make sure the police don't pick him up – keep him to ourselves at the moment."

Amanda got into the back seat of the car and slammed the door behind her. She cursed and lit a cigarette.

George was finished issuing instructions and got in the car. "Okay, ma'am, what now?"

"See where the cars are."

"Still heading north, ma'am, making slow progress, but still five or so miles from each other."

"Let's move in their direction."

The car sped off. Amanda decided it was about time that George received a fuller briefing. "George, this could be a long day."

"I'm at your disposal, Miss Barratt."

"What has Nick told you?"

"Very little, ma'am. He mentioned that you were following up on a couple of murders."

"Yes, a couple of operatives who were apparently retired some years ago. Anyway, they were controlled from my directorate, actually by a man called Gerard Gaines. He's the body at Cookham."

George was a good listener, especially as he drove the car rapidly through the London traffic. "Mmmm."

She went on, "The girl we're picking up works for me also and, I think, so does the killer of Gerard Gaines." When summarised in this way, Amanda concluded she was running a dysfunctional department, but the driver didn't comment on that. Instead, he made a contribution to the analysis.

"And you think the girl's gone after him?"

"Maybe."

George was on the radio again. A voice announced that Alpha was now fifteen miles away, still heading north, with Beta ten miles away and moving in the same direction.

"Will I stand down the others now, ma'am?"

"Yes, we'll get support locally if we need it."

George said to the radio, "Thanks, we got them now." He broke a red light touching eighty miles an hour and they joined the northern convoy.

Chapter 30

The Longtown grapevine was as efficient as ever and everyone knew that a second body had been found. Not everyone knew whose body it was, but that didn't stop them speculating. Val Fraser hadn't gossiped to anyone in the last few days. In fact, she hadn't left her house. This was what one was meant to do when one's partner was murdered. She didn't care about doing the right thing and she wasn't in mourning either. It was strange, but she could hardly remember his face. His clothes and a few possessions were still in the house, but already very little of Lennon endured in the house. It was a house, but it had never been a home.

That hadn't mattered in the first four years when, maybe, they were in love.

She laughed mirthlessly. Bobby had thought himself larger than life, but in death he was already almost completely forgotten. Only the police and miscellaneous public officials cared now, but to them he was just a name.

Love, she reflected. *That was a laugh*. She vaguely drifted back in time. He had been a handsome man once. How had she ever imagined that they could make a life together? She shook her head and helped herself to a large vodka. Alcohol wasn't much of an answer, but she couldn't think of anything else, and it tasted good. She perked up a bit. Lennon hadn't been much of a partner and she didn't miss him, but, on the upside, he had no other living relations, so she now had quite a lot of money.

The house was owned outright and she had been surprised to learn that Lennon's bank accounts sat at a surprisingly high level of credit. More than that, he owned a big share in a local company. As to the company's worth, she had no idea, but it had to be something; after all, it had been around for years.

She knew Adam Jardine and she liked him. He was gentle and decent. He wasn't all that exciting and he didn't have much star quality, but Val had had more than enough of that. This shareholding was also a stroke of luck; it allowed her to get out and, hopefully, meet someone who would make few demands and someone who would understand.

Val Fraser got into Bobby Lennon's car. The mirror and the default radio station were easily adjusted. The seat was too far back and it smelled of him. She lit a cigarette to freshen the atmosphere.

She drove through the town, grateful that no one waved at her, and headed onto a windy B-road. A sign at the side of the road indicated the way and, although the German saloon struggled on the incline and loose gravel, she pulled in and carelessly parked in the site car park.

There were three temporary site buildings and she straightened herself and, without knocking, entered the largest one.

Adam Jardine sat at a desk paying no attention to the papers in front of him. She moved a couple of paces towards him. "On your own?" she asked.

"Yes. I sent them home."

She nodded. He looked dishevelled and strained. Perhaps this would be a difficult business meeting. She took off her coat and hung it on a crude-looking stand. He was fidgeting and seemed unable to speak.

She didn't know anything about business either, so she delved into her bag and located the few papers that detailed Lennon's shareholding. She put them on the desk and laid them in front of him. She hadn't realised that he needed reading glasses these days. He reviewed the files. "Aye, that's the right papers. But what does the solicitor say?"

She sat on an unsound plastic chair at the side of his desk. "It's fine. Bobby didn't have any living relations and years ago we made wills in each other's favour. He says that executory should be a formality – three or four weeks. Meantime I can proceed pretty much normally."

Jardine looked at her. "What do you want to do, Val?"

She said, "Well, I know nothing about the construction business."

"Do you want some tea or coffee?" He rose and made his way to a table which was home to a well-used, but less well-maintained, kettle and some dirty-looking mugs. He inspected about six before selecting two. He was out of milk but she took it black anyway.

Luckily, she didn't want sugar either, so he was able to make two coffees and he returned and placed the mugs on the desk.

"How have you been?" he asked.

Whether she was sick and tired of bottling up her feelings or she just trusted him, she plumped for telling him the truth. "All right really. To be honest, I don't feel anything for him at all."

If Jardine was shocked at this or by the steely features which backed this statement, he didn't show it. He nodded. "Aye, I feel that as well. Sad, really, I knew Bobby a long time. We were friends once. I wonder what happened to him?"

Val said sharply, "Christ, are all men fools? Bobby ridiculed and despised you for ten years and you say that."

He looked up at her and said softy. "Well, it's what I think. Besides, he's dead now. He's going to be dead for a long time."

She reached across and touched his hand briefly. "Oh, sorry, Adam. I just can't be as good as you. I just can't remember any good times."

"You were happy with Bobby once, Val. You had your pick and you chose him."

She didn't look at him. "Where were you, Adam? I mean when Bobby was shot?"

He looked at her and leant upright and back into his seat. "What kind of a question's that, Val? You thinking that I killed him?"

"No, no, don't be so fucking silly. Of course, I don't."

His voice was softer now. "So, why are you asking me?"

"Oh, I don't know. Emma Dixon will be asking around. I like Emma but, damn, she's so fucking good at her job. She'll get to the bottom of things. Everything."

"Aye, I'm sure she will, but it's nothing to do with me. Other than today, I've been on site every day, dawn to dusk, and there's dozens of folks who can confirm it. I've already told her that."

Val said sharply, "What else did you tell her?"

"Well just the truth, about the business. How things were."

"Just the business?"

"Just the business." He fiddled with his coffee mug then got back to safer ground. "So," he said, "do you want to sell these shares or not?"

"What are they worth?"

"I offered Bobby half a million pounds, which I expect you know."

She whistled. "No, I didn't know. Jeez, that's a lot of money."

He agreed. "Well, that offer still stands."

It was more money than she had ever imagined having, and it was tempting.

She reached into her bag for cigarettes. He didn't smoke, but he pushed a dirty saucer towards her. She lit it, took a couple of puffs and laid it down on the saucer. Then she got up and moved to the door. "You sure that the guys won't be back?"

Jardine said, "No, no. I gave them a half day."

She nodded and clicked the door lock. Turning towards him, she noted that he was standing up too.

"I don't think I'll sell those shares, Adam."

He had been trying to buy them for five years, but this time the refusal to sell didn't upset him. The Portakabin wasn't large, and with two strides each, they were standing very close.

A second later they fell deep into each other's arms and both of them kissed and basked in a moment they had both dreamt about for many years.

Chapter 31

Peter Miller wasn't green-fingered. He hated gardening, and his small and dilapidated greenhouse was a mess. The promised grapes were nowhere to be seen and the four tomatoes which had emerged were jaundiced and unappetising. He reached for a spray and gave them a blast without expectations. A medium-sized spider emerged from behind a plant pot; it relocated casually to the far end of the wooden shelf and returned to its work.

Peter envied the spider. It was focused on web-building and keeping comfortable and, with these tasks proceeding satisfactorily, all was well in its world. Peter's world was not going so well, and he was having a lot of trouble working out how to fix it. Nothing he could say to himself was convincing him that his wife had not had an affair with Bobby Lennon. He told himself that the past was the past. Lennon was dead and he didn't need to know. It was easy to say, and it might be that he could cope, but it was really the present and future that he was struggling with.

She knew that he loved her and she knew that he would forgive her anything. So why didn't she just get it over with? Tell him that it was a single indiscretion, it had meant nothing. There would be a bit of hurt, but surely, she must know that they would get over it and he would forgive her.

His unsettled brain raced illogically. Had she loved Lennon? Was she in mourning for her lover? This would be bad, but if she could get over it, so could he.

Lennon was dead and Miller didn't care, but he wondered who had killed him, and that question prompted a whole new set of speculations which Peter Miller liked even less.

He completed tending to the greenhouse plants and abandoned the garden. Without returning to the house, he walked across the golf course and onto the sandy bay. There were a few folks happily pottering on the sand. He resented their happiness. It was a fine day with extensive views, but he couldn't get his head up. After about a ten-minute walk he cleared the last of the beachcombers and arrived at a little-visited part of the bay that was dominated by long grasses and irregular high dunes. A few minutes later, after a stumble on a steep dune, he decided that he had walked far enough.

He sat on a rock and looked out to sea. The day was cloudless and the sea was calm. In the distance, some far-off islets were free of cloud. It was pretty good work from God and Miller had no complaints. He had no complaints about his life either. Born well, expensively educated and a fulfilling and rewarding career. More than that, he had been blessed with love, albeit late in life. And then it had changed, although *he* hadn't changed. He should have spoken to her, but he just hadn't known how.

Would it have made a difference? Probably not. There was nothing surprising in the fact that a forty-year-old woman might be more attracted by someone her own age rather than himself. He was over sixty, and today he felt it. It might not have been surprising, but that didn't soften the blow, and he was hurt more than he had ever been.

He knew she had spent time with Lennon in the last few years. Once he had followed her. A trip to visit a friend turned out to be two days in a hotel with Lennon. That was several years ago, but it had happened again. Why hadn't she just left him? That sort of thing happened every day. It was strange. Despite the absences, on her return she had been little changed and seemed still to be happy.

But she had mourned when Lennon had died. Miller wondered if she would have mourned for him. He doubted it.

Worse, he was finding out things about himself and he didn't like them. They said that you found out about people in adversity and it was true. Peter Miller was having a tough time, and it was just as tough finding out and accepting how weak and insignificant his response was.

The ocean water lapped and broke on the rock below. It was a long drop to the deep green water. For an instant he enjoyed the feel of a light breeze on his face, but it wasn't enough. Peter put his hand into his jacket pocket and fingered the Browning pistol. It was steely cold and it was heavy. He didn't know much about guns, so he removed it from his pocket and laid it alongside him on the rock. He looked out to sea again.

He had reduced his options to a couple. He could either throw the gun into the ocean or he could shoot himself.

He didn't know for sure that his wife had killed Lennon, but it was possible. He would forgive her that, and while that wasn't in his gift, maybe he could help her. Anything but losing her. He didn't care whether he lost her to another man or to the police; either way, she would be lost.

She had lied when telling Emma Dixon that she had been at home most of the day that Lennon died. He had given up golf early that day and returned home. She had been missing for several hours and, on her return, had offered no explanation. Since then she had behaved so strangely that he could only conclude that it was somehow to do with Lennon's death.

He looked up and sucked in a couple of satisfying breaths of sharp, salty air. He reviewed his options. On a personal level, shooting himself was a decent plan. Irrespective of whether God would be there to receive him, one shot would end this pain. Maybe he was a coward, or was it a vague urge not to leave her at this time?

Either way, a quick bullet to the brain didn't immediately appeal to him.

As for the gun, he didn't really know whether it had been fired, but it needed to disappear. The sea was the best place for it and Miller had chosen a decent spot. The tide was out about as far as it could be. The rock he sat upon pushed out about half a mile into the bay, and even at ebb the ground below was never dry.

It was time to do something. He wanted rid of it now. If he waited, there was every chance that he would change his mind and shoot himself. She might not miss him if he were dead, but it was going to be tough concealing the gun once he was a corpse. For all he knew, she might even be accused of killing him. It wasn't much of a legacy. He rose, picked up the gun, and gingerly edged his way to the end of the rock.

The gun was heavy, but he managed a throw of some distance, and it broke the water with the deep splashing sound which told reassuringly of deep water.

Chapter 32

Emma arrived at Jack's villa some ten minutes before the scheduled call with Amanda. Jack was a bit disappointed; he had hoped for longer to chat with her.

They sat in the kitchen and she accepted a coffee. There wasn't going to be much time for small talk, so he didn't start.

"Any developments?" he asked.

She shook her head. "Nothing more at the moment. Perhaps your boss has got news?"

"Maybe." He supped his coffee and lit a cigarette. Jack had a few things that he wanted to talk to Emma about personally but nothing professional, so he said nothing and looked at her instead. He wondered if she was resentful about Amanda's role in her investigation. It didn't look like it.

"Is your phone charged?" she asked.

He'd forgotten about that, but when he looked it was fully charged. And then it rang.

Improbably, the reception was excellent, and Amanda came through loud and clear.

"We're both here, in my house," Jack said with a vague nod to secrecy.

"Anything new your end?" Amanda asked.

There wasn't, and Emma said so.

"Yes, I expected nothing. Your local problem may not be so local after all."

They waited.

"I've had a killing at my end now. Gerard Gaines. I'm afraid he's one of mine also. Long-time MI1 man. Actually, he's been acting head of the directorate for a few years."

"Not much of a start for you," Jack interjected, then realised how insensitive it had been.

Amanda admitted it, however. "No, not great. Anyway, I don't have the full story yet, but here's where I think we are. We had an active surveillance unit and it was decommissioned, only it wasn't decommissioned. In fact, I think it was kept operational, unbeknown to the operatives, and it was, how would you say, *privatised.*

"I think it may have been controlled from my directorate, probably by Gaines, perhaps supported by others. I think the unit had run its course – maybe it was going to be exposed and someone decided it should be wiped out, decommissioned in such a way that there would be no trace."

"Not a bad idea," Jack said. "Quite enterprising."

"And Lennon and Brannigan?" Emma asked. "Were they operatives?"

"Well, that would fit what we know at this stage," Amanda said.

"Did they know there had been a change in management?"

"I have no idea, but thinking about the way these cells operate . . . if you have the same Control, why would you know there had been a change? That was the beauty of the plan. Gaines controlled them when they were official and carried on, just with different sponsors."

Jack blundered in for an early close. "So, who's been killing who?"

"I don't know."

"Gaines?"

"Doubtful," Amanda said. "He may have been involved at first, but if I wanted rid of all the evidence, I imagine Gaines would be part of the problem. Consider – he knows everything. Every operation, every target."

"So why would a private employer want this?" Jack asked. "I mean, what sort of targets?"

Amanda was dismissive. "Well, it's quite obvious. Information is power. Rivals in business, political opponents, folks you want dirt on. Really, the list is endless, Jack."

Told off, he retreated to safer ground. "So, are we finished here? It sounds like a Whitehall problem now."

There was a short pause and Amanda said, "In one sense I think that's true; however, there is a bit more to it than that. The good news, if there is any good news in this fucking mess, is that I think I know who killed Gaines."

They were all ears. Amanda certainly knew how to tell a story.

She admitted in apologetic tones, "Another one of my own, I'm afraid."

Jack decided not to comment upon Amanda's department again.

Emma said hopefully, "So you can pick him up and then ..."

"Well, I could, but you will understand that I'm keen to get to the root of this. I don't believe this assassin is at the head of this."

Emma said, "So what do you want us to do at this end? Just tidy up and hand over?"

"No, no, there's a lot more to do, I'm afraid. I'm in a car at the moment in, you might say, a kind of pursuit. I am tailing two cars at the minute. I need to see where they are headed."

"Who's in the second car?" Jack asked.

"Well, that's another one of my own, but I don't need to complicate things at this stage."

Emma actually laughed out loud at this point.

"Yes, sorry," Amanda said. "I'm just trying to test this theory – sorry to use you as a sounding board. Let me describe them."

Amanda took quite a long time describing Julian Johns and Natasha Gold. Emma and Jack's part in this affair was far from over, he realised.

Amanda confirmed this. "I'm telling you this because it might be that they are headed towards you."

"Here? What for?" he asked.

Amanda had an answer for this also. "Well, I believe that these active surveillance units consisted of three persons."

Jack and Emma looked at each other. Emma said, "So there's a third person, and you think that this person's here?

"It's possible."

Jack persisted. "I still don't see why you just don't pick up these guys. Surely you know how many were in the unit? What about your records?"

"Records are not always kept when it comes to this sort of thing. And, of course, remember this unit was decommissioned officially about ten years ago."

Emma got to the heart of Amanda's plan. "So, you want to tail this assassin or assassins and see who is going to be killed next?"

Amanda admitted that was her plan.

"How far away are they?"

"About fifty miles."

"So, they could be heading anywhere?"

"Yes, that's possible. Look, we can handle this. If they come to Longtown, we have them boxed in – very few ins and outs."

"Yes, but this needs to be carefully handled," Emma said after a glance at Jack. "I mean, we don't want another killing. This is a risk, a big risk. I understand that government, or you, Amanda, want this closed. I understand that maybe even it's best if the entire unit's wiped out. Never existed. But what about down here?"

This was quite a tough question.

Emma leant nearer the phone. Jack walked away and refilled the mugs with coffee. He lit a cigarette. He already knew the answer.

"Yes, there's a risk," Amanda said.

Jack returned to the phone and had a go. "You were able to identify Lennon and Brannigan as former operatives. Can you not at least identify anyone round here who was attached to your department?"

Amanda dampened his enthusiasm. "It's easier to identify dead people, Jack. So much more information. We are looking, but to be honest, I'm not hopeful. At least this way, Johns will lead us there."

Jack had a last go. "So, if your man comes here – *if* – have you got any clue at all who he's after?"

"No, not yet. Emma, can you close up the town? Cover all exits and entrances?"

"Yes, well, Longtown's not London," Emma said. "There are only two ways into Longtown; we've got three squads in town and two entrances."

Jack said hopefully, "Do I have to do anything?"

"No, not at the moment," Amanda said.

"So, are we to expect two cars or one?"

"Probably one, but I'll update you on that. The first driver, Johns, is a killer, that's all I think I know at this stage." Amanda's voice became more serious. "Listen, Jack, I'm confident we can do this, but remember that Johns is a very dangerous man. He's an administrator now, but he was in special forces and various operational teams. He won't ask questions, he'll kill first. He's got another advantage. He knows exactly where he's heading, and he knows what he's going to do."

Most of this Jack knew, but it was sobering hearing it stated in this way.

"Emma, will you excuse me a moment. I need a word with just Jack."

Jack took the phone and turned off the speaker. "Listen," Amanda said, "you've done this sort of thing before and Emma hasn't. I like her and she's a first-class officer. Look after her."

"I thought it was the other way around?"

"Yes, well, it was: but not now. Let me speak to Emma."

He passed the mobile to her. This conversation was a little bit longer and Emma smiled as she shut down the call and returned his phone.

"What did she say?" Jack asked.

Emma covered a couple of points on logistics.

"What did she say at the end?"

Emma put her forefinger to her lips and smiled. "She said that I was to look after you." She laughed. "I think Amanda likes you, Jack."

He decided to ignore this and said, slightly cheesily, "Well, we can look after each other."

She held his gaze for a moment. "Okay, let's do that."

Jack looked at Emma. She looked up to the task and confirmed this opinion by efficiently spending the next ten minutes making phone calls and assembling local resources.

This done, she laughed and said, "Your boss, is it always like this?"

"Quite often, I'm afraid." He added with cynicism, "On the upside we know, or think we know, quite a lot more, apart from the big things like who killed Lennon, who killed Brannigan and, of course, who's the third man – or woman?"

Emma laughed a bit more and was then serious again. "Assuming we can stop this guy, then at least we'll have the third person, hopefully alive."

Jack was unsure. "Even so, they might know nothing about the top guys."

"Maybe, but he or she will at least know about the operations and, of course, we might be able to establish whether or not they killed Lennon or Brannigan."

Jack hadn't thought about this point.

"The third member might have done the local killing and is now surplus to requirements."

It was possible. He said, "We should have asked Amanda about that. I mean whether the guy heading here was in the area at the time."

She moved through to the lounge and sat heavily on the sofa. He sat opposite. She shut her eyes for a second as if weary and then opened them wide. "How good are you with these?" She indicated the guns on the table.

Jack said, "Proficient, perhaps, but no marksman."

"Were you in the military?"

"No, but I've been on several what are described as active missions – I'm sort of like a reserve, like you have special constables."

She looked doubtful. Then she asked the question you were never meant to ask. "Have you ever killed anyone, Jack?"

Normal protocol was to answer this question vaguely, or not at all. He said, "Two, two people."

She looked hard at him. "Did they deserve it?"

Jack opened his mouth, reflected. "That's a tough question. I'm not God so I can't be sure, but at the time, I thought so."

She relaxed her expression. "Do you still think that?"

Jack clasped his fingers together and took a few seconds to answer. "Yes, I think so."

She nodded and looked away for a moment. "Sorry, I shouldn't have asked you that."

"It's okay. What about you?"

She started. "Do you mean have I killed anyone?"

"No, no, I meant how proficient are you with guns?"

"Oh, well, I've been a firearms officer for about five years but there's not much gunplay in these parts. I can shoot pretty well in theory, but …" The sentence fell on her lips as she added with a humourless laugh, "In fact, when I found you over Lennon's body, that was the first time I'd ever drawn a gun in anger."

"I'm surprised," Jack said. "I've had a few guns pointed at me" – he shivered involuntarily – "often by experts. I didn't guess."

What did Emma make of him as a partner? His experience was limited and highly irregular. It was true that he had been recommended by Amanda, but this had been because of accident of circumstances and when the enquiry seemed little more than routine. Now they were engaged in stopping a dangerous and experienced killer.

He wasn't worried for himself, but was suddenly overcome by what might have been a feeling of responsibility. What if his failure got someone killed? More specifically, Emma? He screwed up and shut his eyes and expelled this thought.

He got up and returned to the kitchen and she joined him. They sat at the small table. They were quite close. Her blue eyes weren't sparkling today, and she looked tense.

"Anything wrong?" he asked.

"No, not really."

He accepted that as an invitation to follow up. "Go on."

"Well, I just keep thinking this is all a bit out of my league."

Jack looked at her and touched her arm. "All I can see is a highly competent and professional police detective."

She dropped her eyes. "Yes, I've done okay so far, but nothing like this."

Jack said, "Everything you've done, you've done well. Right? You're a detective inspector and you're not even thirty."

She looked at him and, in flat tones, said," Yes, I suppose so."

Jack liked her, but was reasonably sure that wasn't clouding his judgement. "For what it's worth, I've got a lot of confidence in you. Not that I'm hugely experienced either, but I've seen a few things and met a lot of people. You'll be fine. You're smart and strong and you do things for the right reasons. Trust me, Emma, you can do pretty much anything you want to."

She still looked unconvinced.

He flicked her arm casually. "Look, Amanda obviously thinks so. She's got you looking after me."

This prompted a wintry smile in response, and he realised that she was going to take a lot more convincing.

He rose, returned with a gun and laid it on the table. She produced her own.

"Snap," she said, and they looked in silence at the guns for a moment.

From outside, the sound of a car spraying gravel was followed by a firm knock at the door.

"I need to go back to town for about half an hour," she said. "Get a few preparations started."

He followed her outside.

"Jack, this is Gavin."

He shook the teenage constable by the hand. "I'll give you a call if I hear from Amanda again," he said.

Jack turned on his heel and went back towards the house, but something made him turn, and he watched Gavin reach down to Emma and give her hand a long and gentle squeeze.

Chapter 33

Left alone, Jack was thinking about Emma, speculating more about her personal life than their professional assignment. He knew a bit about her, it was true, but he was sure there was plenty he didn't. She was funny and she was good company and she seemed to like him. What did he want from her? He didn't know; he just knew he enjoyed being with her. It was a start. He wondered how many rivals he had. Dozens probably. She underplayed things, but she was a very good-looking girl. She knew everyone in the town and they would all know her. He wondered whether the young constable was a rival. Workplace romances were common, but surely Gavin was too young for her.

Jack vaguely acknowledged a cliché about age being no barrier. Maybe that was true, although usually the man was meant to be older.

Peter and Suzie Miller were separated by about twenty years. That said, they seemed far from happy. Whether that was anything to do with the age gap or whether it was down to the current enquiries, he didn't know.

He thought about Amanda. At least she was about his own age. Set against this, nearly every time he met with her, someone ended up dead. This sort of thing was tough on relationships.

It was time to stop thinking about age and about women. He needed to speak to his architect, Moore. It was an employer's right to choose the timings of meetings, but when the last meeting had ended with a dead body and Jack being taken to the police station by armed police, he decided that an explanatory phone call was required.

"Sorry for the delay in getting back to you."

"No problem, Mr Edwards."

Moore began to chatter enthusiastically about windows and doors. Jack let him talk. In truth, he was finding it difficult to regain whatever enthusiasm he had once had for the project.

"I'm not going to be able to get down today," Jack said. "Not sure when I can."

"Are you still, er, helping the police?"

Jack laughed. "Yes, but not with their enquiries."

Moore was apologetic. "No, no, of course not."

Jack put Moore's mind at risk. "Don't worry, please carry on with the project. Oh, and I have had a look. There's a couple of payments due for the next phase. Right?"

"Yes," Moore agreed nervously, and launched into a long list of forthcoming activities.

Jack wasn't really listening but he let him finish. "I've transferred the money requested, and a bit more, which should cover everything."

In truth, this was probably all that Moore wanted, and the call ended. Moore had his money and Jack was free to focus on the case.

He started immediately. He had plenty of reservations about Amanda's plan, but there was at least one good thing about it. There were so many official agencies and full-time personnel on the case that he was confident he wouldn't be directly involved. But careless thinking cost lives, and Jack wanted his life to continue.

He returned a Glock to the side table alongside its newer model. He picked up the new model that he had been sent some months back. The new gun was similar in design but it was smaller and he didn't like it. He had never used it in anger, although when it had been issued, he had attended what had been described as an intensive refresher course. Emma was right. Shooting at dummies and targets wasn't the same as shooting at a person. Targets didn't shoot back.

He put it back on the table and picked up the old model. It felt more familiar and he liked it better. He put each of the four magazines in and out several times. He wondered why Britain had to use an Austrian gun and he didn't have an answer. He noted its seventeen-round capacity and replaced it on the table, hoping that whatever happened, he would discharge none of them.

The phone rang.

"Right, Amanda's called," Emma said. "She's about twenty miles out of town now. It seems certain that they're coming here. She's coming to the police station. You need to come over."

Jack located his car keys and picked up a pistol, and then he was outside.

He headed to his car but was halted by the sound of a powerful car approaching fast. His head followed the sound and he watched as the car drove into the villa three doors down. It was Lennon's car. Val Fraser jumped out.

About fifty or sixty yards separated them, too distant to exchange verbal greetings. She hadn't seen him anyway, and he watched as she retrieved a coat and a bag from the passenger seat. She then made her way round to the driver's door, which allowed Jack a good look at her. She was casually dressed, and gone was the worn and tired face of yesterday. Her gait also looked different today. Positive and confident, even purposeful. Whether this fleeting assessment was correct he couldn't be certain, but as she looked across and straight at him prior to going into her house he could be certain of at least one thing.

Whatever Val Fraser was feeling, she was no longer in mourning.

Chapter 34

A four-hundred-mile drive was not what Natasha had expected, but she wasn't tired, and, lost in thought, the hours had passed quickly. Once she had phoned in the car registration, it had been very easy to follow Johns. She still had friends in the agency.

Like so many Londoners, Natasha had never been in Scotland. It was certainly different. Of the many contrasts, only the road network concerned her. Traffic was light, which was good, but the road was narrow, potholed and rarely straight. This was a problem because, ahead, Julian Johns was driving fast. Very fast.

Natasha wasn't a bad driver, and the car she had borrowed was powerful, but it was proving difficult to close the distance. It stood at some fifteen miles now and she was losing ground. How come men never needed to go to the bathroom? She had been forced into two rapid stops. She had no answer to this and, responding to a straight in the road, floored the accelerator.

The advantage of a long pursuit was that you had time to think, time to plan, but the disadvantage was that you risked changing your mind. Her new boss was almost certainly trying to change her mind. There was half a dozen missed calls on her phone. She didn't want to be disturbed, and thoughts of revenge still powered her along the road.

Whatever she was doing, her new boss would not give up, especially as Natasha had stood her up in London. That had been a poor move. She couldn't justify it, but she didn't care right now. She also didn't care that in a fair contest she would be no match for Julian. It was strange that she still thought of him as "Julian". Whatever his name, and irrespective of the match-up statistics, she knew she was going to kill him.

The speedometer kissed one hundred miles per hour, free-fell to thirty, and then rapidly back to eighty. It was fast but it wasn't fast enough. A better driver in a long black saloon screamed past. This was how she should be driving today. An unannounced sharp bend came into view. Ahead, the brilliant red brake lights of the black saloon flashed.

Natasha lost concentration momentarily. When her attention returned, she was on the apex of the corner. Just ahead, the rear lights of the black saloon were still brilliant red. She slammed down on her brakes, about as far as they could go. They stopped her just in time.

She cursed. The black car had slowed almost to a stop. She checked the rear, then side mirrors. In both, the view was the same; two identical saloons had her in a box.

She thumped the steering wheel with clenched fists. It hurt. There was a knock at the window. She shut her eyes and felt a tear of frustration. The two tall men in suits had guns, so she accepted their invitation to get out. She was forced face forward against the car and frisked by another man who was enjoying his work more than strictly necessary. Expertly, he located and removed her pistol and clips, took his hands off her and shouted, "Okay, clean now, ma'am."

This done, he got into Natasha's borrowed car while another large man led her to the end vehicle. He opened the back door.

"Hello, Natasha. Get in," Amanda said.

Natasha's solo pursuit was over.

Chapter 35

About twenty miles further ahead, Johns' BMW was proving to be the right car for the job. Traffic was light and the car gripped the road tenaciously. He was a fast driver normally, but today he had wings. Reckless speed and reckless overtaking didn't really matter when you were heading to commit a murder. He flung the car into another bend and effortlessly passed a slow-moving touring vehicle.

Julian Johns enjoyed his work, especially this sort of assignment, but still cursed Bobby Lennon. If you wanted a job done properly then you had to do it yourself. Ultimately, this was no bad thing because Johns was the best. But the plan had not gone as it should. The scope had increased and the timings had been brought forward. Nonetheless, he was relaxed. He had managed things well. He would execute the commission and he would emerge unscathed.

In a perfect world there would have been more time to kill Gaines, but there had been no choice. Gaines had been a weak link and he had collapsed. It was certain that he would have talked – sooner rather than later. Johns wondered why people were so weak. Why couldn't they control themselves? Guilt, perhaps, whatever that was.

Maybe Gaines could have been helped. Maybe he wouldn't have talked. But it didn't matter now. Now he would never talk. Johns was pleased Gaines was dead. Gaines was old and he was puffy. It had been a long time since Gaines had made a difference, if ever.

Johns knew that *he* had made a difference. The resignation of a British prime minister and with so much dirt on major public figures he had raised the art of blackmail to a point where it seemed like legitimate influence.

With power came money, but this wasn't his primary concern. Money was fine, but only to reinvest in pursuit of yet more power. That's what Johns craved. It was all that he craved. Not in pursuit of a cause, either. He wanted power over people. It was his only high, better than status, money or sex. Smashing the feeble defences of the lazy and self-important was a sweet pleasure.

He didn't know where this urge had come from. He was a privileged only child of upper-middle-class parents and had enjoyed an idyllic childhood in rural Berkshire. Private school, Cambridge and then, through his late father's connections, a run in the special forces, and straight to the Foreign Office on the fast track.

He had loved only once – his parents, but they had died when he was twelve, both of them unexpectedly and well against the odds. That was half a lifetime ago and he didn't miss them now, but he had no complaints either. What was the point? As a songwriter once declared, people were just particles of dust orbiting the sun. If you subscribed to this cosmic view, it didn't really matter if you killed people. If you wanted to change – and Johns didn't – you could, of course, try religion. It didn't have all the answers, but it did accommodate mystery.

He wasn't convinced. He didn't believe in religion and he didn't really believe in anything other than the present. This didn't include sex. He never thought about sex, and he didn't need companionship. Then he had met Sir Hector Laing, the only man Johns had come close to admiring. He was wealthy, urbane and intelligent, but none of that impressed Johns. What *did* impress him was that Sir Hector made a difference. He had global influence and had the phone numbers and the ear of almost every person of influence. That was what Johns wanted, and he was close to it.

He looked at the digital display and was satisfied with his progress. The town was less than half an hour away. Not that he was in a hurry. There was plenty of the summer day left. He was on a planned break, and although he didn't have a perfect plan, that didn't really matter. He had managed to kill Gaines easily enough, and this one would be just as easy. He knew where he was going and, when there, he would be able to improvise. No one knew he was here and he would be in and out quickly.

He wasn't reckless, however, and he had a couple of safety plays in mind. Longtown wasn't London or the Home Counties. There was no reason to risk standing out. Strangers were noticed here. But he had a plan. He slowed the car to a halt and allowed himself a moment of relaxation.

The views were good, but they didn't do anything for him. He had visited this region before, but it wasn't familiarity that made him indifferent. He hated places like this and he didn't understand them. Nothing happened in these places. Why did anyone live here? He shook his head. Only professional reasons had brought him here previously and, tedious as these visits had been, the upside was that this experience and knowledge was helpful.

The Canish airbase had once been a very large facility, at one time the biggest in Europe. It had closed about a decade ago and created economic depression in the region. Johns didn't care about that. What mattered to him was that literally hundreds of empty buildings had been left behind. Many were now dilapidated, and a few had been re-let by the local government in a miserable attempt to turn the place into some sort of Enterprise Park. This had proved to be an extremely limited success, with the result that Johns had been able to lease, not in his own name, a well-constructed and well-secured unit as a local and very well-hidden resource.

Johns slowed the car some ten miles short of Longtown and pulled off the A-road and onto a poorly maintained single-track road. It continued for a couple of miles but he met no oncoming traffic. The track split – improbably –into two separate and even narrower tracks. One of them led to a reception in a secure area, but the other allowed for anonymous entry into the heart of the disused base.

He chose the latter and moved slowly along undefined road and eventually onto firmer ground – the former runway, which led to the buildings.

All was quiet when Johns arrived at his lock-up. It was a large double-skinned brick building with an angled roof. He produced a key and entered through a wicket gate. Once inside, he quickly slid the main door halfway open and drove his car inside.

There were two other cars inside the unit, both unlocked and with keys inside. This was a good start. Beyond, the unit was shelved and sparsely filled with miscellaneous items. Johns walked to a small partitioned office area.

It wasn't extensively furnished and had a desk and a couple of uncomfortable seats. There was an old-fashioned heater and a kettle with some dried-out instant coffee in a jar alongside. There was no chance of a café latte here, so he didn't bother.

At the end of the office there was another door. This led into an empty room about a dozen feet square with a concrete floor and a manhole cover. Johns reached into his pocket and produced an irregular piece of metal that, when twisted into the manhole cover, allowed him to lift it and slide it clear. He knelt, leant down and after a short fumble located the light switch. Light burst from the hole and revealed a tight-fitting spiralling set of stairs.

Johns was in great shape, and he easily worked himself onto and down the stairs, flicking away some dust that had attached to his trousers. The basement store smelled musty but it was dry and well appointed: the best room in the lock-up. On a modern desk sat two computers, a telephone and a variety of communication and surveillance gear. Against one wall, a rack with a wide range of clothing items, and on the far wall, a collection of the latest and deadliest modern weapons.

Johns took down a couple of handguns and selected a Browning. He didn't like the Browning, but it fitted in better in Longtown. There was plentiful ammunition in a strongbox on the floor, and he put gun and clips on the desk. He reviewed the collection again. There were three machine pistols, two assault rifles and a sniper rifle. He lifted the sniper rifle. With this, he was proficient, but although he knew the area, he did not know it well enough. It was satisfying to kill someone from a mile away, but for this to work, the firing area had to be carefully pre-selected, and he hadn't done that.

As a superior alternative, he selected a Benelli shotgun. It was adaptable and worked in a variety of situations. It was his favourite, most recently tested at the front door of Gerard Gaines. This model was in better condition than the one he had, and besides, he needed to use a different weapon. He laid it alongside the Browning.

Satisfied with this firepower, he reluctantly acknowledged that a change of clothes might be prudent. His first selections proved ill-fitting and uncomfortable, and he was forced to select some old-fashioned Chinos and a polo shirt, both bearing labels of an unknown designer. Sacrifices had to be made, however, and he re-ascended the basement stairs and returned to ground level.

He left the office and reviewed the cars: a Swedish estate car and a German saloon. Bland was the order of the day, so he selected the estate and he threw some items from his car and the shotgun inside before covering them with a far-from-clean travel rug. This done, he conducted a last review of the available items on the metal racking, but there wasn't much else he needed for a routine murder.

As he turned to leave, Johns noticed a set of golf clubs leaning against the wall. The set was modern and in good condition, and the pockets of the bag were full of golf balls. He was a mediocre golfer and didn't enjoy it much, but it did give him a vague idea. He lifted the clubs and a set of shoes that looked about his size. There were a couple of woods in the set and he elected to lighten the bag by ditching them. He kept one of the headcovers, and in a few moments, he had locked up and was heading for Longtown.

Chapter 36

Amanda waited for Natasha Gold to compose herself. Luckily, she wasn't in a hurry, for it took Gold two drinks and five minutes to get started.

"Sorry, I don't know what I was thinking," she said.

Amanda had no idea either, so she waited.

Natasha tried again in stuttering tones. "I-I expect you think it's all wrong?"

Amanda was unclear. "Which part in particular?"

"G-Gerard and me."

"Were you lovers, or business partners, or both?"

"Lovers. We lived together. What else?"

Amanda looked at her closely. Running mascara wasn't enough to convince her of anything. "So, you worked and lived with Gerard for two or three years. Why should I believe that you weren't involved?" It was a harsh question.

"I didn't know anything," Natasha said desperately. "I can see how that's tough for you to believe."

It certainly was. Amanda said, "Surely you must have known, or suspected, that something was wrong."

Natasha looked desperate and could only repeat, "No, no, I don't know anything." Her features hardened. "All I know is that he's lying dead in Cookham, and that little fucker killed him."

"You were in the house at the time?"

"Yes. We were sitting together having a drink. Working things out."

"What happened?"

Natasha seemed in partial control of her running eyes and nose now. "He hadn't come home, you see. He had been a bit down for a few days. I knew he would be there. It was the last bit of his parents' estate. He always went there when he was low. We were talking, just talking, and there was a knock at the door. Gerard went to the door. I was sitting on the sofa." She looked up and her lip trembled. "I remember the next few seconds clearly."

Amanda knew Natasha would remember them for the rest of her life, but she said nothing.

Natasha bit on her lower lip and finally steadied it. She breathed in deeply and audibly. She managed the next few words without breaking down. "I ran to the door. Gerard was dead."

They sat in silence for a long time. Amanda waited until Natasha felt able to move on.

"I looked out the door, and—"

Amanda needed to get some structure in the next bit. "Did you see Johns immediately?"

"No. Not at first, the road turns. He must have been moving quickly."

"So, how did you catch up?"

"I ran to the corner, fast. He slowed down as he got to his car."

"And you saw him clearly?"

Natasha's eyes blazed. "Crystal clear."

"And you saw the registration number?

"Yes."

"Had you seen his car before today?" Amanda asked.

"No, never."

Amanda nodded. "Did he see you?"

Natasha shook her head. "I'm sure he didn't."

Amanda gave her a few seconds. "I know you took a car, but what were you doing in the time between leaving Cookham and taking the car?"

Natasha looked skywards. "I need to talk to that garage."

Amanda didn't manage to suppress a laugh. Having not yet been cleared of murder or criminal conspiracy, this was the least of Natasha's problems. "I'm pretty confident the garage will be okay. I had a quick chat with the owner. I told him you were an agent and it was an emergency. He was happy to cooperate, and besides, he'll get his car back and some money for his trouble."

She returned to the main theme. "So, between Cookham and the car?"

Natasha was suddenly very calm. She turned, and this time held Amanda's gaze. "I went to kill him."

"How did you know his home address?"

"I'm the head of HR, I know everyone's home address."

It was a good answer. "So, the story you told me over the phone," Amanda said. "Obviously I got most of it, but we need to go through it again. We've got plenty time. The story Gaines told you about the surveillance unit . . . why was that troubling him?"

"Well, these deaths, Lennon and the other one. He thought someone was targeting the unit and maybe he would be next. Also, he told me that he had made a lot of money for the unit and all he could foresee was, at best, no more money and, at worst, exposure or maybe death. He was in a bad position."

She added slowly, "And I'm afraid he owed a lot of money – gambling, I think. I didn't know about that, either."

"He had no idea who was doing the killing?" Amanda asked.

"No, none."

"He mentioned no one else?"

"Well, the government minister, as I told you. Not his name but I think he might have met him recently."

Amanda tried again. "No other names?"

Natasha shook her head.

This was essentially the story she had blurted out in the earlier telephone call. In truth, Amanda wasn't much further forward.

"Where is he?" Natasha asked.

Amanda hadn't cleared Natasha yet, far from it, but she put her hand on her arm. "We're close to him. Don't worry, I'll get him."

Natasha looked round and her eyes were blazing as she said, "I want to be there."

Amanda shook her head. "No, sorry, that just can't happen, Natasha."

In reply, Natasha uttered a short series of single unconnected words.

"We're not in the revenge business, and," Amanda added brutally, "I still don't know for sure that you're not involved in this fucking mess."

Natasha was either a fool or a liar, or maybe she was just in love. Amanda didn't know too much about love, but she knew it made people do stupid things. She tended to avoid love herself – she wasn't sure whether that was by luck or design. It was why men like Jack Edwards were useful.

It was tough to fall in love with Jack. She liked him and sometimes he was fun, and once, a few years ago, she had thought about sleeping with him, but it was difficult to take him seriously. His instincts were mostly well intentioned and, although he took a bit of persuading, he usually got things right. She suspected that the times they were together might be the best of him. It wasn't a reassuring thought.

Her driver broke in with an update. "Target's stationary, ma'am."

"How far?"

"Five miles away."

"Okay, tell them to follow us in."

Chapter 37

After a short uncomfortable drive over narrow potholed roads, Amanda bid her driver stop. She turned to Natasha. "Stay here." She got out and conducted an impromptu conference with her agents. "No change?"

"None, been static for ten minutes, ma'am."

Amanda looked out over the dozens of storage units. "Okay, let's have a closer look. Send a couple forward."

The radio crackled. "In position, ma'am. Clear sight, twenty yards or so. All quiet."

"Observe, keep out of sight. If the target moves, do not intercept. Radio for further instructions."

The voice on the radio signalled understanding.

Amanda turned to another man. "Right, get these cars away from this road. Keep out of sight but as close as you can. Don't intercept unless essential. Ideally, I want to know where he's heading. I'm going into the town to see the local inspector. It's about three miles away. Radio me if he moves."

Five minutes later, Amanda arrived at the Longtown police station. The front door was opened promptly in response to a rasp from a silver button. Constable McDonald was a tall, overweight man of about fifty-five. "Detective Inspector Dixon's not here, ma'am. You want me to call her up?"

Amanda nodded.

He did so. "She's just talking to a few of our guys, making sure that they have everything clear and in the right position. She says she'll be here in about ten minutes. Would you like a cup of tea, ma'am?"

She said that she would and asked for two more after bringing her driver and Natasha Gold into the office.

"How long have you been here, Constable McDonald?" Amanda asked.

"Charlie, ma'am."

"I'm Amanda," she returned.

"All my life, Amanda. I was born here and I've been a policeman, oh, more than thirty-five years."

"Always here?"

"Yes, I could have moved, but you know, there's not a lot of applicants for posts around here and, well, I like the work and, of course, I know everyone."

"That certainly helps. Do you know why I'm here?" she asked.

"A little, ma'am. I mean Amanda. I've had a couple of chats with the inspector and she briefed us all on the man you're chasing."

Amanda thought that Emma was wise to have "chats" with McDonald. She would learn more from McDonald than from all the lecturers at Hendon.

"So, as for the man we are chasing, as you put it, we are keen to know whether he has any contacts or associates here," she said. "Our man was known to Lennon and Brannigan. We are probably looking for a third person. Someone with a communication background. Worked at the base, maybe."

McDonald said, "Aye, I've been thinking about this. It was a big base and it was full of spies. And in the old days there were a lot of comings and goings with Northern Ireland."

This was all known to Amanda. But then McDonald added a little bit of value. "Theoretically it could have been lots of people, but it probably had to be someone who is still local. I mean, it could have been someone from elsewhere but, well, Lennon wasn't often out of here and, you know, he was a close one." He took a sip of tea. "And if it's someone here, then it had to be someone Lennon knew. As I say, he didn't spend that much time with many folks, and Emma's spoken to most of them. So has your man, Mr Edwards, I think."

In response to another rasp from the buzzer, McDonald admitted Emma and Jack. Emma looked professional but Jack appeared edgy. After shaking Emma's hand, Amanda, in a breach of protocol, gave Jack a hug. He responded a bit and she enjoyed it. They went into a small office space whereupon Amanda led an impromptu conference.

A large-scale map on the wall had a few pins stuck in it and Emma confirmed they represented the location of her roadblocks. "We've got every part of the town covered. Not a huge job."

Amanda stood up and pointed. "That's where Johns is. Five minutes north."

"Unit number 139," Emma said. "It's in Lennon's name."

Jack spoke for the first time. "How long has he been at the lock-up?"

Amanda glanced at her watch. "About twenty minutes now."

Jack nodded. "Well, you know that his car is there, but how do you know *he's* there?" Glances were exchanged around the table. "If he's not there, he might be killing someone as we speak. Have you *seen* Johns?"

Amanda frowned. She looked to Emma. "What do you think?"

Emma shrugged. "It's a long drive just to spend time sitting in a lock-up."

Chapter 38

They disembarked at the edge of the airfield. Amanda left Natasha Gold in a car with an agent. In silence, she cautiously led them to the place where she had left her spotters. They still reported no activity.

Amanda made up her mind. "It's time we took a closer look. We need to get a good position, but I want just one person to go to the door. If he's in and we go mob-handed, it's over. So, who are we going to send?"

"What about seeing if there's someone in the reception area and sending them?" Jack asked. "I mean, that would be best."

Amanda agreed, but rejected the suggestion. "No, we can't risk it – Johns is capable of anything. I want the whole story here, but I didn't come here to get a civilian killed."

"I'll go," Emma said. "I'm local. Just a policeman checking around."

Jack opened his mouth but then shut it again. He looked uneasy and Amanda understood why. But it was the best option. There was a quick consultation about the cover story – something about stolen goods – and then everyone except Jack and Emma drew guns.

After a jog to an adjacent unit and a short series of movements, everyone was in place. In response to a nod from Amanda, Emma headed towards the door. They watched her knock on the wicket door lightly then wait. Nothing happened so she tried again, louder this time. When a third effort also drew no response, Amanda broke cover and beckoned everyone else to follow. They were all out of skeleton keys, but the wicket door yielded after three or four flat-footed kicks.

Three gun-toting agents burst through the wicket door in single file. "Clear, ma'am," came a cry and Amanda, Emma and Jack followed.

There were two cars in the unit, an office and some well stocked shelving. The forward agents confirmed the office was clear. Amanda and another man checked the cars. She pointed at one of them. "That's Johns' car." She kicked a panel so hard it made a dent. "That's what we have been tracking."

There was no need to ask where Johns was. They had no idea. He could be on foot or have acquired another vehicle. He could have already killed someone and gone out of the area.

***

Amanda and her fellow professionals were still poking about in the car, and it seemed to Jack they were taking too long. There was no chance of immediate action, because now there was activity in the office. Jack had nothing better to do, so he followed Amanda. There were four people staring at a manhole cover while another was grunting with a crowbar. Jack drifted back into the small office, and at last was able to add some value when he spotted a manhole hook that had been deposited in a coffee mug. He rushed through and announced his finding. This saved some seconds and the cover was lifted then slid aside.

Jack might have been able to squeeze down the narrow stairs, but three was already a crowd. Amanda and Emma returned after a few minutes.

"Well?" Jack said.

Emma looked serious, and Amanda said, "Johns is not going to be short of guns. It's like a quartermaster's store down there."

Examination of the floor beside the cars created a consensus that there had been another car here recently, something to do with fuel stains and near-invisible rubber markings.

This was all very interesting, but it yielded no clue to Johns' whereabouts. Amanda said as much in a general address. She would leave a two-man reception committee within the unit to cover Johns returning and the rest of them would return to the Longtown police station.

Concealment was no longer important, but speed was, and Jack trailed the others in a sprint back to the cars.

Emma checked in with her patrols and drew a blank. She threw down the radio receiver. "Nothing."

As the three cars sped back to the town, Jack, Amanda and Natasha in one of them, a mobile conference was carried out. The existing checkpoints were to be maintained, and Amanda, Emma and the agents would split and undertake roving patrols in the town.

"What am I to do?" Jack asked.

Amanda said, "I want you to go back to your villa. Take Natasha please. There'll be a roadblock into Canish. There's just one access road, I understand?"

It wasn't much of an assignment, but things were now too serious to argue. He nodded. Time was of the essence, and Amanda had to brief Jack on Natasha while they all travelled in the car together. "Jack, Natasha works for me, but not on the operational side. She's here because she has some knowledge of this particular operation."

Natasha said nothing. Jack had questions, but he didn't ask them. "She has had a long drive and needs to rest," Amanda added.

Jack watched as Natasha nodded weakly. It was clear that this girl was in a state of shock. He wished Amanda had left her in the police station.

Jack and Natasha got out of the car at the villa. Amanda beckoned Jack to return and he stuck his head back into the car. "Take care of her, Jack. Gerard Gaines was her partner. She was with him when he was killed. She was coming to kill Johns."

This explained some things but not everything. Before he could fire a supplementary question, Amanda leant forward and kissed him lightly. "I'll see you later. Be careful."

Jack and Natasha leant on the wall and watched as Amanda's car carried on past the villas and stopped at the hotel at the road end. It pulled into the hotel car park. There were a few cars there and she stood with a radio, presumably checking up on them. She did the same at the adjacent golf club car park.

He turned to Natasha and led her into the villa. He hadn't wanted to get involved in a gunfight, but he hadn't sought a role as a glorified babysitter either.

She was nearly as tall as he was, but she looked very small and very vulnerable when sitting huddled on the sofa, her head bowed.

"Can I get you something?" he asked. "Tea, coffee, a drink of something else?"

In a low voice, she said, "Thanks. Tea."

She clung tightly onto the mug he handed her and took a few sips.

He had no idea what to say so he said, "Amanda said you have had a long drive. There are four rooms upstairs if you want to lie down."

He picked up a few clothes that were strewn on a chair and added, "I'm on holiday. This is a holiday house, so all the rooms are prepared."

"Yes, maybe I will."

It was difficult enough to talk to anyone about a bereavement, but discussing the murder of a partner that had happened that day proved impossible for Jack, so they sat in silence.

She finished the tea and accepted a top-up. This was concerning, for the tea seemed to be reviving her. She would want to talk. And she did. "Have you ever lost anyone close, Mr Edwards?"

Jack figured that she wasn't talking about parents and grandparents, so he didn't mention them. His problem was that he *had* lost someone in the category she was talking about. And, against all odds, she had also been murdered. He was very well placed to talk to her about this sort of loss, but he didn't want to. It wasn't the time to tell her that every day for the rest of your life you would think about it. Mostly it was okay, but the pain never went away. It was also important that he didn't tell her, at least today, that when a relationship ended in this unnatural way, it was never closed, and moving on, as other folks gently recommended you do, was not easy. You had been in love with that person and you stayed in love with them forever, even though you wanted to stop. You just couldn't do it.

He wasn't going to tell her all that now. "No," he said, and added, "Look, why don't you have a nap? I'll listen out for any news and I'll wake you if there are any developments."

She hesitated, but she was exhausted, and an involuntary yawn clinched the argument. He led her up the stairs, and after checking that the second-largest room was in order, he left her, saying that if she needed anything just to yell.

He returned to the lounge and was sure that she would sleep. Looking out of the window, everything was normal. What were Amanda and Emma doing?

Chapter 39

Amanda and Emma had lost their quarry, but that didn't mean there was nothing they could do. They sat in the Longtown police station. Amanda took a phone call and turned to Emma. "We think Johns was in London, certainly on the day of Lennon's killing, and the same with Brannigan. When exactly did Brannigan die?"

"Still waiting on the doctor," Emma said. "Two days before Lennon, provisionally."

Amanda nodded. "So, we've got a local assassin or another out-of-towner."

"Maybe someone here kills the first two in the cell and then Johns comes for them?"

Amanda agreed. "Sounds reasonable – well, at least possible. I mean, if someone wants the cell eliminated, they're going to go for everyone. No loose ends."

"So, our local hunter might be the hunted?" Emma asked.

"Maybe,"

If it *was* a cell-on-cell killing and both assassin and victim were guilty, it would be easier to live with the consequences. A local solution might even be better and give the whole case a more sanitised solution, but that was as far as it would go. Whatever was happening in this sleepy Scottish outpost was initiated and being directed from London.

Emma was reviewing the local position. "Well, anyone could have killed Lennon, a man or a woman, but." She shook her head. "Brannigan, well that had to be a man."

Amanda put up a token objection. "It doesn't take much force to put a knife in someone's neck."

Emma apparently didn't find that convincing. She shook her head again. "The man was a misfit – no known friends. No connections that we can find. Hard to imagine him allowing anyone that close."

"Jack said you had a bit of a shortlist locally."

"Lennon's partner, Val Fraser," Emma said. "She hated him, so did the neighbours, Peter and Suzie Miller, and they both worked at the airbase." She paused and added, "Val Fraser, she's a friend of mine, but the word is that she is quite close to Adam Jardine."

"Who's he?" Amanda asked.

"A local businessman. He worked with Lennon. He hated him too."

"Popular guy."

Emma continued, "Jardine's in the clear. He's got about a dozen witnesses over the last few days. Fourteen-hour shifts on a building site."

"And the others?" Amanda asked.

"No real alibis. Riding, golfing, all on their own when Lennon died. But that's just where I'd be if this was purely local and it was just Lennon. I mean, none of them really knew Brannigan as far as I know. Either way, we've got an assassin who we can't locate and someone local that he's after."

Amanda nodded. "At our end, I'm having every record checked to see if we can find anyone with an MI1 connection with local connections." She saw Emma perk up and grimaced. "Well, apart from the fact that records were irregularly kept, if at all, most are not computerised and, remember, this was a long time ago, in a unit that wasn't supposed to exist. I'm looking for someone else, actually an ex-government minister."

Emma took this bombshell in her stride. "How is he involved?"

"I don't know for sure. I was told he was, but I need much more. Anyway, he's missing too and I can't find him."

Amanda looked at Emma and knew that they were thinking the same. At present, there was nothing to do but concentrate locally.

"Let's get out of here," Amanda said. "I'm sick of sitting around."

Emma agreed and they went back to the car. They conducted a round of the checkpoints, but learnt nothing.

"No word on these local suspects of yours?" Amanda asked.

Emma said wryly, "Seems I keep mislaying folks too."

Joking helped Amanda, but not that much. Someone was going to get killed, and it was going to be her fault. She had seniority and she was sure that her approach to the case would be understood at the highest levels. That was all right, but it was cold comfort. There was going to be a long lessons-learned session at the end of this case, for sure.

She withdrew from her reflections at the same time as Emma, without indicating, lurched the car into the car park area of what passed for a supermarket in Longtown. There were a few spaces, but Emma abandoned the car in the main thoroughfare. Amanda followed her out of the car and was able to pacify some irate shoppers while Emma returned to the car accompanied by a woman.

Voluntarily, but without looking happy, the woman got into the back of the car and Emma into the front, whereupon she drove out of the car park and again parked illegally, half on and half off the pavement. She turned off the engine and introduced Amanda to Mrs Suzie Miller. The woman in the back seat was tallish and slim. About forty and pleasant-looking. She also looked composed, as if sitting in the back of a police vehicle under these circumstances was a common experience.

Suzie Miller asked no questions but looked at them quizzically.

"Amanda's from London," Emma said. "She's in the same line as I am. We have a problem and we're keen to speak to you. As you know, we're investigating the deaths of Bobby Lennon and, as you've probably heard, a Mr Brannigan."

Suzie Miller said nothing.

"Well, there's a man in town – he came from London and we think he's here to kill someone else."

Suzie still didn't say anything. She was certainly a cool customer.

"We have no reason to think that this concerns you, Suzie, but meantime we are just alerting anyone that we have spoken to about Bobby Lennon. I asked you this before, but is there any reason someone could be looking for you, Suzie?"

Suzie gave this question slightly more thought than Amanda thought an innocent person would need, but this was offset by her response. Her face expressed neither concern nor deceit. "No idea, Emma. No idea at all."

Emma set a feeble trap. "Do you want protection at the house?"

"Why would I need that?"

"Why indeed?" Emma returned.

Amanda had a last go. "Is there anyone else that you think might need our protection?"

Suzie shook her head. Amanda wasn't really satisfied. Usually folks were guarded in the presence of authority. Suzie Miller wasn't.

"Where's your car?" Emma asked.

Suzie indicated the car park.

"You heading home now?"

"Yes."

"We're heading out to Canish. We'll tag along. Help you with the guys at the checkpoint."

Suzie didn't demur and, after an uneventful five minutes, the cars pulled up at the entrance to the village in front of a marked car employed as a crude roadblock. Emma got out and spoke to the policemen. After a short conference, she waved Suzie through.

Emma returned to the car. "Nothing. What now?"

Amanda was out of ideas, so Emma turned the car and they headed back to town.

Chapter 40

Jack stared out of the bay window of the villa, indifferent to the view. Natasha Gold was asleep upstairs. That was good, because he didn't want to talk to her. She seemed a nice person, but he needed a break from handing out condolences. He wondered what would happen to her.

Amanda was a fearsome enemy but also a formidable friend. She would help Natasha, but only if she wanted to be helped. That was never certain after such a catastrophic loss, but she was young and had a chance. It was true that Natasha was a member of the security services, but a job in human resources couldn't have prepared her for the sight of her lover being ripped to bits by a shotgun at their front door. What could?

He lit a cigarette, opened the window to freshen the room and surveyed the scene. All was normal, all was quiet. Two golfers were teeing off at the first hole, a challenging opening shot with the Irish Sea covering the entire left-hand side of the hole. It was a golf course with an international reputation. A course you had to play before you died. He laughed. These days it seemed that if you came to Canish, you improved your chances of dying.

The two golfers started well enough and they proceeded down the fairway and out of sight. This left the golf course, dunes and bay free from people, save for a single golfer who was occupied in a small practice area at the nearside of the course. Jack was, or at least had once been, a decent golfer. Out of practice, certainly, but still better than most hackers.

The practising golfer was in the right place. Jack enjoyed an entertaining few minutes watching as the golfer produced a full repertoire of doubtful shots, before soft sounds behind made him turn. Natasha Gold was in the room.

Although her hair was dishevelled, she seemed to have recovered some confidence and composure. She sat down without speaking and he brought her another cup of tea. He didn't sit down opposite her but returned to the bay window and continued looking outside. He knew she would speak if she wanted to.

His idle vigil continued until the peace was broken by the sound of a car that contained Suzie Miller. She pulled the car into her drive and opened the hatchback. She delved in, lifted out a couple of bags and went into her house. She returned for the rest of the car-load.

The practising golfer had given up on pitching and was now focusing on his long game. He reached into his bag and took out a club, which he uncovered. There was no practice swing, and after a short fiddle with the club, the golfer jogged towards them and leapt over the boundary fence of the golf course.

Jack must have uttered a sound, for Natasha now stood alongside, sharing his view.

The golfer was moving rapidly now, and a second or two saw him across the narrow road and arrive at the ungated entrance of the Millers' villa. He stopped for a second and pointed the golf club forward. The golf club looked like a shotgun.

Natasha screamed. "That's Johns!"

Jack turned, picked up a Glock and crashed out of the front door. Johns was a professional, and he wasn't rushing things. With slow, deliberate strides, he advanced towards Suzie, who had not yet registered the danger. Jack was only a semi-professional and he was rushing. Two strides out of the front door, he pointed and squeezed the gun twice. He tried again. He needed a lucky shot, but it didn't happen. Johns turned for an instant and casually returned a single barrel from the Benelli shotgun in reply. It was a better shot, and the burst hit Jack – or so he thought.

Jack fell heavily to the ground and rolled over twice before being roughly halted by the immovable stone dividing wall. He had no idea how badly he was injured, but he wasn't dead. Death, however, wasn't far away. If he sprung to his feet and presented himself, the shotgun would finish the job. Sitting cowering under the wall wasn't much of an option either.

Jack wasn't a hero, but in response to the sound of quickening footsteps on the gravel next door, he decided he might as well die with his boots on. He leapt up. He was lucky. Johns, perhaps having seen him fall, was focused exclusively on his primary target. The shotgun was discarded at his feet now, and his handgun pointed straight ahead a few feet from Suzie Miller's head.

She turned and faced him. Either she couldn't or she didn't want to run. Her face was passive and neutral. Jack had no time to wonder why she didn't look scared. Johns was very close now, close enough to make certain.

It was a difficult shot and well against the odds, but Jack went for it with unsteady hands. As the Glock discharged, he knew he had missed. Another gunshot exploded a second later. Jack cursed. He had not saved Suzie Miller. He felt a rage overpower him. He wouldn't miss Johns this time.

Before he could fire, slowly Johns' knees bent and he fell over sideways and hit the ground with no attempt to break his fall. People only fell like that when they were dead. With an effort, Jack clambered over the wall.

Johns had a hole in his head, which was all the confirmation he needed.

Suzie Miller was still standing. She didn't look great, but she didn't look dead.

Jack's head was spinning and, for the first time, he became aware of a throbbing pain, which he provisionally judged to be coming from his shoulder. He ignored it and frantically turned detective. Suzie Miller didn't have a gun; Jack had missed at least four times, and there was no one else. So that left Natasha Gold.

She was leaning on the wall, wearing a smile that was maybe a sneer. At her feet, on his side of the wall, was a pistol. He felt a surge of admiration for her accurate shooting, but his adrenalin was ebbing away. There were things to do.

He inched over to Natasha and, with caution, vaulted the wall, bent down and picked up the gun. She said nothing and continued to stare at the body of Julian Johns.

Helpfully, Suzie Miller also remained passive, although she had at last moved, albeit only a yard or two back from the dead assassin, and was now sitting on the ground against the house wall.

Jack picked up Johns' shotgun and pistol and, now loaded with guns, conducted a cursory panoramic review of the scene. There was no one else around. He sprinted into his house and found his phone. He rushed outside again, and everything remained in order. Amanda answered. He blurted a few words and she got the idea. He leant against the wall, with his Glock still in his hand, making sure that the two women remained in full view.

He rubbed his shoulder gingerly and his hand picked up a reassuringly small amount of blood. He didn't like to tempt fate, but he figured he might live. He helped himself and Natasha Gold over the wall to the Millers' side and they both sat and leant back. Everyone waited for what seemed like a long time.

The silence was total. In Canish, it was quite possible to have a gun battle on a late summer evening without anyone noticing.

The cavalry took only a few minutes, and Amanda and Emma arrived to a scene untouched since Jack's phone call. They were accompanied by two other vehicles and about half a dozen men. All the new arrivals were armed. As Amanda entered the driveway, Jack threw down his gun alongside Gold's pistol and Johns' shotgun and handgun, making a formidable discard pile.

Amanda holstered her gun and knelt beside him. "Are you okay?"

"I think so," Jack said and pointed at his shoulder.

"That looks all right. Is that all of the guns?"

Jack nodded. He was very tired now. She squeezed his arm. It felt good. When you died, you missed these sorts of things. Jack returned the squeeze and briefly and fairly lucidly explained what had happened and what he had been doing.

Amanda nodded and deputised suited agents to return Natasha Gold and Suzie Miller to their respective houses.

"It's not over yet, is it?" Jack asked.

She didn't lie and admitted as much. "At least we know who the third man, or woman, is now." That was true enough. "No thanks to me," she added.

He let this go. They both knew that, at best, things had not gone to plan.

Amanda looked at his shoulder and insisted he remove his T-shirt to allow for a closer inspection. After a moment, she called a paramedic over. "Can you dress this? I don't think it's too bad." The paramedic was more thorough, although rougher, than Amanda, but shared her conclusion. The liquid stung as the wound was cleaned and a bandage applied.

"Are you sure that's okay?" Jack asked. "Do I have to go to hospital?"

"Do you *want* to go to hospital?" the paramedic replied.

Jack admitted that he didn't. "Aren't there pellets in there? Aren't they poisonous?"

Amanda laughed and held out an open hand. "This was in there – just." She slipped the single pellet into a plastic bag and sealed it.

Emma joined them and sat down at Jack's other side. "Johns got a single shot to the head from Jack's Glock 19. A good shot." She indicated the weapon from amongst the arsenal lying on the ground.

Amanda looked serious. "Careless, Jack, very careless, but very lucky. Lucky for you Natasha Gold's a good shot, and lucky she's as innocent as I think she is."

She was quite right. He said, "Sorry, the other gun was on the table. I didn't have time to put it away. I looked out the window and Johns was there."

Amanda tutted but moved on. She pointed at the shotgun. "Jack was shot – well, winged – by that one." She went through the rest. Johns' handgun hadn't been fired and, after an inspection of the magazine, Jack's gun had been fired four times.

Amanda rolled her eyes upwards. "Four shots?"

"Four misses," Jack corrected. He decided to move on. "What now?"

"I want to speak to Suzie Miller," Emma said. "She's alone and I want to question her before her husband gets back from golfing."

Chapter 41

From the elevated eighteenth tee, Peter Miller assessed his final drive. In the early evening of the high summer, the golf course was a great place to be. The breeze was light and the sun still had some heat. The tourists were finished and back at their hotels. He had the expansive links to himself, and he was playing well. None of this made him happy. Only Suzie mattered. Getting rid of the gun had been a good idea, but what else could he do? He had no idea. He just wanted her back, and anxiety was overwhelming him to the point of insanity.

He hit the ball. When you weren't worrying about golf, it was easier to play well, and the ball sailed high and straight down the fairway. He threw the bag over his shoulder and followed it. If you were any good at golf, quite often there was a long walk between shots, and Miller had about two hundred and seventy yards to walk. It was difficult, no matter how depressed you were, to have your head slumped on your chest for that distance, so when it rose, he looked across to his villa. He wondered if she was home. Having about six cars sitting outside the villa was wrong. He stopped. The golf bag slipped from his shoulder and he started to run. Normally, he would have had to break such a journey to gather breath, but not today. Each desperate stride nearer the house increased his fears. In less than a minute, he was inelegantly clambering over the wire boundary fence. He was saved from falling on his face by a man in a suit about half his age. The younger man didn't need assistance, but Miller noticed he had help available in the shape of more armed people than Miller had ever seen.

Miller couldn't speak, although he tried.

The man in the suit helped a bit. "Mr Miller?"

Miller managed to nod.

"There has been an incident, Mr Miller. Your wife is unhurt and is in the house." Miller put his hands over his face. "Thank God. I need to see her now."

The younger man wasn't quite so helpful this time. "She's giving us a statement at the moment. You can see her when that's done." He put his hand on Miller's shoulder and, despite his further protests, expertly directed him into the back seat of a car.

Chapter 42

Amanda sat in an armchair opposite Suzie Miller with Emma and Jack supporting from the sofa. Despite everything, Suzie Miller was composed and silent.

Amanda started at the top. "Can you tell us why this man came to murder you today?"

Suzie Miller shook her head vigorously.

This was Amanda's second encounter with Suzie Miller, and it seemed that not even a brush with death could draw her out. Amanda tried again. "Do you know the man? The assassin, I mean?"

Suzie spoke for the first time. "No."

Amanda believed that could be true, so she helped her out with more information. "Your attacker's name was Julian Johns. He works for British Intelligence, MI1. A rogue agent. We believe he was coming to kill you. Have you heard of him?"

Suzie Miller could only manage another shake of her head.

"I expect confirmation soon, but I believe you were an MI1 agent too, in a surveillance operative."

Suzie found a sense of humour. "That's classified."

"I'm glad to hear you say this, but as I'm the director of MI1, you can safely trust me." This time, Amanda decided not to bother waiting for Suzie to say nothing. "I'm going to work on the assumption that you were, Mrs Miller. Two of your colleagues,

Bobby Lennon and Patrick Brannigan, are already dead. At the moment, I don't think that you killed them, but I don't know for sure, so you need to convince me."

Suzie Miller went back to silence.

"When did you retire from the service?"

Still nothing.

"Suzie, help us here," Emma snapped. "You're in danger and we might not be here next time."

They waited to hear how much she valued her own life. Not much, it seemed.

"It's hard to see why you won't help us, Mrs Miller." Amanda threw her a bone. "I'm fairly sure that this unit was operating illegally. I can tell you that, at this stage, I am not primarily investigating these activities." It was a qualified reassurance, however, and it still wasn't enough to start the conversation.

"I cannot give guarantees at the moment," Amanda pressed on, "but it's not my focus. I need to know how it worked, who controlled it, details of the operations and, most importantly, whether there are going to be any more killings." Her voice sharpened. "If you don't help me, I can only assume that you have played a bigger part than I think you have."

These threats didn't seem to do the trick either, but at last they found a weak point. Emma rose and idly gazed out the window. "Suzie, your husband's outside."

Suzie features unfroze for the first time and her features softened.

"This could go high, and it's unlikely that he can be kept out of it." Casually, Emma added, "And we'll keep on going and going. Is Peter up for that, do you think?"

Suzie didn't speak, but her lips were limbering up. There was a long silence, and at last she said softly, "Where is he?"

Amanda said, "In a car outside. You know we can detain and question him. Really as long as I decide."

She caught a grimace on Jack's face; he always hated crude use of power. But this time it was going to work.

"Can I see him?" Suzie asked.

"Not until we know more – a lot more." Amanda said.

Suzie took a few deep breaths and a couple of sighs. Then she started talking. "I worked on the local base. Mostly administrative at first. After a while, I got attached to the guys working in Northern Ireland. Well, at that time, it was crazy. Special Branch, RUC, MI6, everyone."

Amanda nodded. She'd heard a lot of stories about the old days.

"At first, I was just typing up recordings of surveillance, then providing a bit of analysis. I can't remember why, but we were short-handed and they took me out on a mobile unit. I think they were surprised. I've always been good with machines. And then they asked me again and that was that."

"Were you always with Lennon and Brannigan?" Amanda asked.

"Yes, right from the start. For a long time, we worked very well together."

"How well did you like these guys?" Emma asked.

"Brannigan was okay. Odd but okay." Her eyes hardened. "Lennon not so much." She paused. "For about twenty or so years, we've been listening into the private conversations of politicians, businessmen, foreign diplomats, even a few celebrities. You know, very little of it was ever interesting. People aren't really very interesting."

"We will want details of that later, but I am working on the assumption that you had no knowledge your unit was decommissioned about ten years ago, and all subsequent operations were illegal," Amanda said.

Suzie nodded. "No idea whatsoever. How could I?"

"You had no direct contact with Control, with London?"

"No, none. Bobby Lennon was the skipper." The dam had broken now and she went on. "Lennon told me about a year or two ago that one or two operations might have been unofficial." She held her hands up. "What could I do other than stay silent?"

Amanda didn't bother with retrospective advice. "Did you ever sleep with Lennon?"

When set against illegal surveillance, political blackmail and murder, this was pretty insignificant, but it didn't seem like that to Suzie. Her fury was instant. She took a bucketful of breath and her eyes blazed. "Once, just once. He said to me that he was safe, but my part in these operations would come out. He said he could protect me if . . . If …"

The words died on her lips. It was certainly a possible motive for murder.

"He was just a rat. I hated him." Then she shared what seemed her only concern. "Don't tell Peter, please. I love him, but I just couldn't tell him. He has nothing to do with this, nothing at all."

"I can promise nothing other than if this fact is immaterial, I won't use it," Amanda said. "Did you kill Lennon?"

Suzie's features hardened. "I wouldn't be sorry if I did, but I didn't."

"Where were you that day?"

"At the hospital getting a check-up."

Emma said, "I think you told us that you were out riding when we last spoke."

"Yes, I did, but I didn't want to talk about the check-up in front of Peter. He worries about me. It's easily checked."

"And how did you get on at the hospital?" Amanda asked.

"All clear."

"That's good. Now, do you have a gun, Mrs Miller?"

Suzie nodded. "Shall I get it?"

"No, where is it?" Amanda deputised Jack to go to the study and locate it. He returned empty-handed.

That was a pity. It brought Peter Miller into the equation, and if that happened, Suzie might clam up again. There was no avoiding the question. "Did Peter know about the gun, and where you kept it?" Amanda asked.

In a household so tidy, there was only one answer.

"Did Peter like Bobby Lennon?"

Suzie said, "No, he hated him. I think he thought I was having an affair with him."

There was another motive. Amanda sighed. "So, you both hated him, both had a motive and your gun is missing."

All Suzie could manage was, "Peter wouldn't have killed anyone. He couldn't." It wasn't much of a defence.

"We are going to have to speak to Peter," Amanda said. "You know that."

Suzie nodded.

Amanda did her best to soften the blow. "I can let you see him, but you will have to go back to the police station for a fuller statement. When you are away, I am going to search this house. I'll be looking for your gun – and anything else that's relevant. When we talk to Peter, we will not tell him about you and Lennon." She added a rider. "Unless it is absolutely necessary."

This plan of action was not negotiable. "Are you ready?" Amanda asked.

Suzie nodded and everyone left the villa. Amanda led. She opened one of the patrol car doors and Peter Miller emerged. Amanda held him back and turned and nodded to Suzie, who ran and wrapped herself around her husband.

Amanda gave the lovebirds a bit of time by conducting a round of short conferences with Emma and the others engaged in crime scene work.

Finally, Amanda collected Natasha Gold from Jack's villa, and with the Millers in one car and Gold in another, some of the circus left town.

Chapter 43

The sun had nearly set over Canish. Jack was a sucker for a spectacular sunset, but it wasn't doing it for him tonight. A reaction had set in, and it was impossible to avoid speculating on the human cost. It was an interesting case, for sure, but not interesting enough to cost the lives of so many.

He poured himself a large brandy. It wasn't so bad for the dead, maybe, because they were dead. Natasha Gold, the Millers, others lived on and were going to have to live with the pain for God knows how long. Someone must surely have loved Brannigan, and then there was Val Fraser. Who knew what she was thinking?

Jack was all right, apart from his failure to get Emma Dixon to find him interesting. He would get over that. He moved his mind back onto the case. He had no thoughts on the London end. It was Canish that interested him. There were several possibilities but not much evidence. Johns was not in the area when Lennon and Brannigan died. It could have been another London assassin, but if that were so, Jack couldn't progress, so he dismissed it.

What about Natasha Gold? Her partner was up to his neck in this, so it seemed reasonable to assume she was involved or at least knew something about it. But she wasn't dead and Johns hadn't been after her. He could have killed her in London. Were they in it together? They were colleagues and they might have been lovers. Natasha had told Amanda the story, and it was her that had put them on Johns' trail. So, not working together, but was Natasha covering her own tracks? Did she have to kill Johns?

It sounded too fantastic and he didn't believe it. If Gold had been acting, he was going to have to quit. No part of him doubted that she was shattered by the turn of events. She had loved Gaines, like Peter Miller loved Suzie. A more realistic theory occurred to him. If the assassin was local, why not Suzie Miller? She was a woman of character and determination. She had been blackmailed into Lennon's bed – why not blackmailed into liquidating the cell or liquidating Lennon?

Jack decided to get into Johns' head. What would he do if his brief was to eliminate the cell? He could, of course, have conducted all the killings himself, but he wouldn't start with that plan. The senior operative in the cell, Lennon, could be trusted. He was local and he was venal. He would accept the commission and carry out orders and, when he was done, Johns would kill Lennon. That seemed safer than making trips as a stranger to an area where strangers were noticed.

Set against this, Jack wondered about something that he *did* know. The killing of Gaines and, indeed, the attempt on Suzie meant that Johns was in a hurry. Had Gaines been cracking?

He shook his head and reached again for the brandy. A thought occurred to him. He got up and searched for his phone and called Amanda. She didn't answer, which was annoying. His annoyance didn't last; there was a knock on the door and it was Amanda. He was pleased to see her and said so. Once in the lounge and under an unrelenting spotlight, it was clear that she also was tired. She was dressed casually now, jeans and a shirt. She wore no makeup and her hair was tied back in a short ponytail.

She flopped on the sofa. "What about a drink?" She liked brandy too, so that was easily fixed. She kicked off her shoes and he let her get comfortable.

"Can I stay here tonight? I've got a bag in the car."

175

Jack got up and she threw him the car keys, which he threw back after returning with her bag. He felt more protective than amorous, although Amanda didn't need any man's protection. They sat in a comfortable silence and exchanged smiles.

"How have you been?" she asked.

They hadn't had a real talk for about a year. Well, they had both been busy, or at least she had. They were both single and probably sexually attracted to each other, but, almost better, they had drifted into a very easy friendship. The sort where you picked up at exactly the spot you had left off without re-finding each other.

He wasn't quite sure why he didn't chase her down. That she was what might be described as a catch was undeniable. She was smart, sexy, single, and they got on well. He wondered what else he was looking for and returned no answer, so he sipped at his brandy and looked at her. "Fine, well, I've been working on the house, a little business and a lot of leisure. You?"

Amanda yawned. "Working mostly." She laughed. "I've just started a new job."

He laughed back and wondered who would get to the point first. Usually it would have been Jack, but he summoned an unusual burst of self-denial.

Amanda asked first. "You met anyone?"

He was pleased that she asked. "No, not much luck in that department."

"Don't worry, there's someone out there."

"Maybe, but you've got to be looking." He returned the question.

She said wearily, "No, I'm on a break from men."

He was surprised to discover that, but it pleased him. She might be on a break, but he doubted men were.

"Concentrating on work," she added. "What about you, you doing much?"

"Not really," he admitted. "I'm a bit bored but I just can't find the right thing. Made a few charitable donations and keeping an eye on the quarry up north." He said, as an afterthought, "Have you got any more work for me?"

Amanda laughed. "I can try, but I'm not sure you're the sort of person that a modern security service can use." She wasn't really joking, either. She had "used" him before, but that was on a needs-must basis, he was certain.

He said playfully, "Well, maybe I could change."

She shook her head doubtfully. "I've been to more meetings on health and safety, equal opportunities and environmental awareness in the last twelve months than about the defence of the realm. Would you enjoy that?"

"Maybe I could provide an alternative view."

"Sorry, there's no room for that nowadays." She continued reflectively. "Trouble with you, Jack, is that you believe in things. Neutrality is what we need, an ability to see all sides."

Jack yawned. "Maybe you're right. Anyway, what about your new department? I thought we had only MI5 and MI6 nowadays?"

"That's mostly true, but a few more still exist, albeit on a smaller and more discreet scale."

Jack said. "So, they are officially extinct but run behind the scenes, a bit like this unofficial surveillance cell, in fact."

She laughed and held her glass forward, which he refilled along with his own. "I've had a bad start," she admitted.

"It's hardly your fault. Less than a week in the job. Will you be okay? Will they fire you?"

She considered. "Everyone knows it's nothing to do with me, but fault isn't always important in my business."

He nodded. There were no set rules in the security services; you just did whatever it took to get the job done. "Have the top guys got your back?"

She narrowed her eyes. "I think so, but really it all depends on how things end up."

"And the best-case scenario is?"

"All of the murders cleared up, no public association with us, and, of course, the end of the cell."

Jack nodded. "Ironic that the people you are chasing have the same objectives as you. I mean, do you know who's really running this? If the cell's been operating for years, Johns was too young. He can't be the boss."

"Hopefully it was just Gaines and maybe another one."

Jack lifted an eyebrow in question.

"David Preece, ex-government minister. Gaines and he worked together."

"And it stops there?

"We will see." Amanda yawned a couple of times.

"You want to sleep?"

She yawned again. "Yes." She forced herself out of the sofa.

"Upstairs," Jack said. "The room with the door open."

She leant across and kissed him softly on the cheek. He felt a frisson of excitement, and thought about following her but, with a big effort, pushed his body down into his seat. It worked, and he stayed seated as she headed upstairs.

Chapter 44

In Canish, the high summer nights weren't long, and the sun and the birds had been up and about for a couple of hours before, at seven-thirty, Jack flicked open his eyes. He was in the chair that he had sat on last night. He put his hand to his shoulder. It didn't hurt. The chair was comfortable, but it wasn't as comfortable as the six-foot bed upstairs. The bed in the next-door room that Amanda occupied would have been more comfortable still.

He got to his feet and made himself some coffee. It was too late to try sleep again, so he went back to his chair and looked out of the window. It was a fine morning. He wondered whether he had the energy to play golf. He lit a cigarette and decided that he didn't.

Senses were returning to his body. Maybe he would take a walk after all. He decided to have a rest while he decided. His dozing was interrupted by the noise of a door slamming. He lifted his head and looked out of the window. The scene was the same as before, except for the figure that now straddled the golf course boundary fence and was heading to the bay.

He went upstairs, conducted a rapid toilet and grabbed a coat. A moment later, he was on the golf course, although the figure was out of sight. He quickened his stride a little and was rewarded by a view of the figure heading round the bay and into a section of irregular dunes.

He was now too near, so he slowed a little, walking just out of reach of the gentle lapping of the clear, blue water. It was relaxing and reassuring, and he continued to amble until he had reached the end of the broad part of the sandy bay.

He navigated a few rough dunes, and the part of the bay hidden from the main road opened into a smaller sandy strip which was ended by a low promontory of rock.

Jack moved towards the rock.

At his approach, Val Fraser looked up. She was well wrapped up against the early morning breeze. Jeans, practical boots and a waxed jacket were local regulation wear. "Good morning, Mr Edwards."

He nodded and decided to keep it formal. "Miss Fraser."

She laughed and said, "Oh – Val, please."

He was forced to reciprocate.

"You are up early today, Jack. Especially as I understand you had a busy day yesterday."

The Canish vine was evidently functioning well. Jack wondered who had told her and, more importantly, he wondered where she had been yesterday. He asked her.

"Oh, I went for a drive to the other side of the peninsula," she said airily.

She looked out to sea and back at him. Her hat was shapeless, even ridiculous, but it didn't look ridiculous on her. He had met her once and observed her from a distance a couple of times. Each time, he had raised his appraisal of her. She was younger than he remembered, and she looked a lot better when not drinking a double vodka and tonic. As she sat on her rock looking ahead, he studied her profile; a more important thought occurred to him, and he began to realise that Val Fraser was a woman of character. People like that were always worth talking to, so he clambered up the rock and sat alongside her.

He looked out to sea. A couple of seals basked on an outcrop. Jack envied them. They were living in the present with full bellies, companionship and the sun on their backs. He doubted they had complications in their lives. Humans just couldn't do that, and it was a pity.

There was no better time to start the interview. "What did you hear about yesterday?"

"Just that there was a shooting incident at Suzie Miller's house. Someone tried to attack her and you killed him."

Jack didn't correct her, nor discuss his missed shots. "That's a pretty good high-level summary. Anything else?"

"Not really. Everyone just assumes that it's linked to the others, Brannigan and, well, Bobby." Her voice was neutral as she mentioned his name. It hadn't been an effort. She was over Lennon, for sure.

"What do you think, Val? Do you think there's a link?"

She didn't answer directly. She turned and looked at him. "Are you a full-time spook, Jack?"

He decided to play along. "No, no." He half laughed, "Is that what I look like?"

She turned her blue eyes on him. "No, I don't think so."

Jack was curious. "Why not?"

She tilted her head and flicked her hair off her face. "Well, you don't seem quite as serious as you ought to be. Besides, you don't look like you are good at taking orders." She looked him up and down and delivered the punchline. "And you're a bit out of shape."

Jack laughed. "Thanks for that."

"So, what exactly is your status?"

There was no avoiding the question. Jack opted for the truth. "I'm a part-timer, a sort of reservist."

She narrowed her eyes. "Are you working on this case?"

"Yes."

"So, who's the boss? Emma Dixon, or that woman from London?"

"Mostly the woman from London, as you call her. How do you know about her?"

"Longtown is a very small place, Mr Edwards," she said.

"Yes, I keep hearing that." He looked at her. "Which makes it odd that we haven't solved these murders yet."

Val raised her eyebrows. "As a part-timer, do you always tell your boss everything?"

"Do you mean do I have to report everything you tell me?"

She nodded and narrowed her eyes. "Yes, that's exactly what I mean."

"Nearly always, to be honest. The key question is what she does with information she receives. In my experience, she has discretion, and I've seen her exercise it several times."

Val looked away and there was a longish silence.

"How about I tell you some things, Val? Just what I think?"

She turned back to him. "Go on."

Jack lit a cigarette and looked out to sea. "We think that three people were targeted here. Your partner, Brannigan, and now Suzie Miller. Two are dead and Suzie is alive. For now."

She was a good listener.

"Basically, we have two problems. Firstly, we cannot place the folks who ordered the killings at the scene for Bobby and Brannigan's killings. They probably had local help."

She didn't react.

"Secondly, we don't know whether there will be another attempt to kill Suzie. The police think that Suzie might have carried out the killings, or maybe her husband."

At this, Val Fraser laughed loudly. "Jack, honestly. Do you seriously think that Peter Miller could kill someone?"

"Why not?"

She shook her head.

"But what about Suzie?" he asked.

"Suzie loves her husband. Devoted to him." She spat out a bit more information. "Bobby screwed her once. Did you know that? He had been after her for years. She hated it and she hated him."

"Why did she sleep with him?"

Val Fraser looked at him and her features narrowed. "I'm going to tell you, Jack. I still don't know if I can trust you, but I'll tell you what I think, sort of off the record."

Jack gave a warning no full-time spook would ever give. "I'm not a journalist."

Val Fraser gave a slight nod. "She slept with him because he blackmailed her. He said he would expose her intelligence activities. At first, I thought it was just Bobby, that's what he did, but then she told me about it."

He had to interject this time. "Why would she tell you?"

The answer was simple. "We're friends, good friends. I've known Suzie for years. Since school."

Jack was gaining in confidence now. "Did she tell you about the intelligence work?"

Val nodded. "Oh yes, Not the details of the operations, but about the arrangement. What she did."

"Did she kill Brannigan or Bobby?"

Val reddened. "No, no of course not!" Her voice lowered. "Mind you, she's a strong woman, Suzie. I think she could have. But I don't think so."

"Why not?" Jack persisted.

"I thought you said Suzie was the target, not the killer?"

"Yes, at the end, but she might have done the early killings. The police think she might have, and they can't find her gun."

"That's not much of a case."

"Maybe not, but there will be pressure to close the case."

Val Fraser wasn't stupid. She looked out to sea wistfully. "Yes, I can see that. So, we need to convince them it wasn't Suzie or even Peter?"

"If they're innocent, yes."

"Oh, they are innocent." She paused again, then said, "Jack, let me run my theory past you. It's just a theory, but it seems to me more likely than your theory."

Jack was excited but didn't want to show it. "Try me."

"Have you got any cigarettes?"

He handed her a cigarette and then cupped his hands round his lighter. She held them and lit the cigarette. She dragged on it a couple of times, and then put forward her theory.

"If someone from London wanted to kill these folks to shut them up, it might be better to hire someone local."

"At first, perhaps."

"Well, if your choice was between Bobby, Brannigan and Suzie, who would you choose?"

Jack thought he knew the answer but said, "I'm not sure. I don't know them well enough to say."

"Fair enough," she replied. "Paddy Brannigan was a nice guy, shy and different, but would you trust a New Age misfit with secret orders? And Suzie, well, she wanted out but didn't know how to. She was sick of it. A gentlewoman who loves her husband." She paused for a second. "And then there was Bobby. Leader of the group, enjoyed his work, cruel and accepts orders unquestioningly."

"So, you think that Bobby was deputised to kill Brannigan and Suzie and they, whoever *they* are, would take it from there?"

"That would be my guess."

"But that's not how it worked out."

"Plans don't always work out."

"So, what went wrong with this plan?" Jack asked.

Her answer was simple. "Somebody killed Bobby before he finished the job."

"So, we are left with who killed Bobby?"

"Yes, if you agree with my theory."

Jack returned to the official line. "Why not Suzie, then?"

"Because Suzie didn't know about the plot. She told me that and I believe her. Besides, she didn't kill Paddy Brannigan." Val spoke as though that was a fact, and after accepting another cigarette, she said, "Bobby killed Brannigan. He was out early that day. When he came back, I heard him confirming to his controllers that he had killed Brannigan and was about to kill someone else. He didn't mention a name, but I knew who he meant."

Jack suppressed a gasp of excitement. This was real evidence at last. "You heard this? How?"

"I heard him on the phone when he came back to the house."

"Careless of him."

"Well, he didn't know I was on the stairs. It was early."

"Did Suzie know this. Did you tell her?"

Val shook her head.

Jack was trying to sound disinterested, but his heart was thumping. "So, someone stopped Bobby from getting to Suzie?"

"Yes, that's my theory, Mr Edwards. Someone who hated him and wanted to stop him killing Suzie."

There was a long silence now, during which they both smoked and looked out to sea.

"So, what do you think of my theory, Jack?"

"It seems to cover some of the facts. Should we try and test the theory, maybe more officially?"

"I don't know," Val said.

"Why not, what does it depend upon?"

She didn't answer.

Jack filled the vacuum with some of his own information. "They haven't got a complete case, but who knows how it will develop. However, there's always the gun. Bobby was killed with a Browning."

Val turned towards him and reached into her pocket. "Like this one?"

Jack couldn't help himself and recoiled a little.

"Don't worry, Mr Edwards, I'll put it down over here."

Jack said calmly, "Is that yours?"

"No, no – it was Bobby's."

He said, with a little reservation, "And why are you carrying it?"

"I'm getting rid of it."

Jack tried his luck. "Will you let me have the gun?"

She laughed. "Afraid not, Mr Edwards," She allowed no time for debate. She rose and threw the weapon into the ocean below. "Well, that feels a bit better. Now it's safe, right alongside Suzie's gun."

"Did you get rid of that one too?"

She was uncharacteristically guarded and said sharply, "No, but I think that's where it'll be. Let's just say that you can see a lot while gazing out to sea. That's pretty much all there is. I don't know what you are going to do now, but knowing it's not Suzie must make a difference."

"Well, I don't know that, or indeed anything else, for sure. Did you kill Bobby to stop him killing Suzie?"

"I hated Bobby."

"Enough to kill him?"

Val laughed. "I don't go around killing everyone I hate, Jack."

"But if you were to find out they were planning to kill a friend?"

She said wistfully, "I suppose that might be different."

Jack worked for Amanda, but his real boss was what was right and wrong. It was tough to condemn Val Fraser, and he wasn't going to, at least not yet. He rose and looked down to her. "We'll talk again."

She seemed satisfied with, this and he headed back to the villa, leaving her sitting on the rock alone.

Chapter 45

Jack walked slowly on his return to the villa, but still the journey didn't last long enough for him to decided his next steps. On balance, he was happier than he had been yesterday. If Val was to be believed, there weren't likely to be any more killings. That was, if Amanda could close things down at her end. He believed in her, but she hadn't been on top of things so far. She would improve.

Although his first thoughts were of Amanda, it might be more of a challenge for Emma. She was tough, but she had local baggage. For all Jack knew, Emma might hate Val Fraser or even the Millers. She might be inflexible, hiding behind duty.

Jack didn't like that sort of police officer, but he liked Emma, so there was some hope. These deliberations looked like being put to the test soon. As he approached the boundary fence, two cars swept past and halted outside the Millers' home.

Surprisingly, both Millers emerged and, hand in hand, went back into their house.

After seeing them indoors, Emma Dixon returned to one of the cars and, to Jack's surprise, kissed the young constable through the driver's window. The car drove off and she looked up and spied Jack inelegantly clambering over the wire fence. She looked a bit embarrassed. Jack hailed her, making no allusion to the kiss. She smiled, perhaps relieved, and followed him into his villa.

As they entered the lounge, it appeared as though Jack had some secrets of his own, as Amanda greeted them barefoot and dressed in a long shirt that looked like his.

She made some coffee and then joined them in the lounge. Emma seemed completely relaxed. He slightly resented that Emma probably had the wrong idea, but he couldn't do anything about it, so he lit a cigarette.

Emma sat and reported her progress. "I didn't find a gun. There's nothing else in the house. I can't hold the Millers, so I let them go." She looked at Amanda. "What next?"

Amanda sat down, displaying a lot of leg. "Carry on looking, testing the statements here, and I'll go back to London and see a few people."

"Yes, fine. Hopefully there'll not be any more action here." Emma offered nothing further in support of this thesis.

Jack, however, agreed with her and wondered what else she knew. For the moment, he resolved to keep out of it. This resolution was broken a few seconds later when Amanda asked his opinion.

"I don't fancy the Millers are guilty, but I can't be sure. There's probably more to be learnt at the London end."

This short assessment was also accepted solemnly. "Okay, Emma," Amanda said. "I'll leave a couple of my guys here, at least for a few days. Use them if you need to. I'll leave you too, Jack." She laughed, and so did Emma, which was annoying. He had done a better day's work than either of them so far, but he flashed them a weak smile.

"I'll leave for London soon. There's a plane at half past nine."

Emma had sent her car back and Amanda had about an hour, so they relaxed and started chatting about nothing in particular. Jack wasn't really involved in these conversations, so he drifted in and out of the lounge until Amanda had dressed and announced that she needed to go.

A drive of five miles took them to an airport terminal about the size of a portacabin, with four of the two dozen car spaces occupied. Jack left Emma in the car and he walked in with Amanda. "I need to talk to you."

She looked surprised and looked at her watch. "Make it quick, the plane leaves in five minutes. Why didn't you talk to me earlier?"

"I didn't know Emma would be with us."

Amanda sat down. Jack made it quick and told her about his morning meeting with Val Fraser.

Amanda considered this information. "And why shouldn't Emma hear about this?"

"Well, Val Fraser had Lennon's gun. I mean, if she killed him, she's had the gun for some time. Emma could have searched the house or something like that. I mean, they are friends."

Amanda got up and spoke to an airport official. "Just holding the plane for a few minutes," she said. "What do you think? Did Val Fraser kill Lennon?"

Jack considered. "I think so."

"And if she did was it to save a friend, or to get rid of an enemy?"

Jack shrugged.

"If you knew someone was coming to kill me, would you kill them, Jack?"

The questions weren't getting any easier.

"So, you think Emma knows this and is shielding her?" Amanda asked.

Jack shook his head. "No, I don't think she *knows* it, but maybe she suspects it."

Amanda said cynically, "The good news is that if Val Fraser *did* kill Lennon, then this thing's at an end locally." She tilted her head as if considering the next step. "Say nothing to Emma at the moment. I need to do a few things in London. I'll call you later." She got up, and so did Jack. She gave him a hug. Customs clearance took about five seconds, and Amanda's plane was in the air before Jack drove his car out of the airport car park.

Chapter 46

After an uneventful flight from Longtown Airport, Amanda arrived in London and got into a waiting car. At least she had an appointment this time. She rehearsed her approach. She didn't have nearly enough. A man like Sir Hector Laing would know that and he wouldn't crack. Some would have called off the meeting, and most would not have sought it.

Sir Hector Laing could make and break careers in an afternoon – and had done so before. His influence was immense, and he had powerful connections in every part of Whitehall. For all of these reasons, Amanda wasn't going to be making an arrest today. At best, she might improve her understanding of the case and even close it down; at worst, her career would be over. She valued her career, but not above everything else. That was probably her only edge. Sickening Whitehall compromises went with the turf, but she had limits.

She entered the opulent portals. This time, the receptionist didn't have to revert to her book of excuses and, in a few seconds, the same senior assistant she had met a few days ago descended the stairs and she joined him in a return trip to the first floor and into a large office.

It wasn't the conference room this time. Sir Hector's lair was large and it was imposing, like the man himself. He sat erect behind an enormous desk and was casually smoking a large cigar. His face wasn't casual. It wasn't hostile but much worse – fixed and confident, the face of real power. He beckoned Amanda into his parlour and, after a self-conscious walk of about the width of a football pitch, she accepted his indication to sit down. She knew he wouldn't leave the desk to sit beside her. He didn't; it wasn't going to be that sort of meeting. When she refused a drink, he waved his assistant out.

From behind the desk, he opened the discussion in a deep, sonorous voice. "Miss Barratt. I am very keen to cooperate with your enquiry. Trust and accountability are essential, even in the most delicate of operations."

She already felt sick. She conducted a final tactical review and then made up her mind. Whatever else was true, Sir Hector didn't seem the sort of man who respected weakness.

"Have you located David Preece yet?" she asked.

"Alas, no. I imagine that he's still on holiday."

She let this lie go unchallenged and chucked in one of her own. "Since our last meeting, obviously I have not been able to interview Mr Preece, but I have found out quite a bit more. Mr Preece is now of primary interest to MI1. Do you know a man called Julian Johns?"

"No."

She didn't believe him. "Well, with respect to this illegal surveillance unit, Johns has been killing off all the members."

"Have you arrested him?" Sir Hector asked.

"No. Mr Johns is dead."

Sir Hector said nothing, but he didn't look displeased. "That is a pity, Miss Barratt. No doubt such a man would have been useful to you in clearing up this case."

Amanda considered punching him in the face. "I don't need Johns. I need the top people. The people that controlled the operation."

"Mr Preece?"

"I don't think so, Sir Hector."

He looked at her quizzically and she played her best shot. "I've got a list of every target of these surveillance operations, every single one. I'm not much of a statistician, but I can link every political target to your own activities – exclusive news stories, resignations, etc. – and I can link all the business targets to positions in your trading."

He looked vaguely interested at best. She moved all in. "Every bit of this information was useful to you and your political and business interests. So, Sir Hector, either you knew and directed these operations or, at best, have been knowingly using information illegally obtained."

He looked as relaxed as ever and exhaled a thick plume of cigar smoke. "Surely it goes without saying that I have no knowledge of any such activities, Miss Barratt?"

Amanda half rose. "You will, of course, say so, Sir Hector, but I don't believe that. And I'm close to proving it."

"Sit down, Miss Barratt."

She sat back down and looked up at him. He rose and joined her on a facing armchair.

"I've heard a lot about you, Miss Barratt. I will tell you a little about how the matter stands. I know nothing about these illegal activities, of course, but the operations you outline may have been undertaken for reasons other than private profit. Have you considered this?"

"Were they?"

"I have no idea, but it occurs to me that money is needed for all sorts of intelligence operations. You talk of black and white, Miss Barratt. Not everything is so clear-cut. The unit was legal and then it was illegal. And sometime it might have been, well, a bit of both."

"Was it?"

He was in total control of himself and smiled. "Well, again, I really couldn't say but, in my experience, there are always grey areas. From what you have told me, I would have said that it is in everyone's interests that we hear no more about these activities."

Theoretically this was true, and she said so, but added, "How would we know that it's all over?"

"Well, it sounds as if it might be. Perhaps Mr Preece will be able to confirm things on his return."

Amanda didn't think so, but let that go. "There may be more killings."

"I don't know, but you told me that there were three people targeted. I understood you to say that they were all dead?"

"No, not all."

If this was an unpleasant surprise to Sir Hector, he didn't show it, and he shrugged this off as a detail and returned to his main theme. "I can only repeat that I know nothing about these operations, and, subject to an interview with Mr Preece, the matter would seem closed. I have given this a bit of thought after our first meeting. Actually, I ran it past someone, an old friend."

If he was looking for favours from connections, maybe she was making progress. He reached over to his desk and pressed a button. From a door beside a bookcase on the far wall, a door opened and then Nick Devoy was sitting alongside.

Devoy said breezily, "Hi, Amanda. Where are we now, close to closing the case?"

Amanda didn't need to recap the details to Britain's top spy. Ultimately, she worked for him and so did everyone else. He would know everything.

She fired his question back. "Do you think we have closed the case, sir?"

"Well, I have asked around a bit, and I've had a meeting with Sir Hector and a few colleagues. It seems that one or two of our predecessors might have employed this agency in the past, even when it was beyond its sell-by date."

Amanda wasn't surprised. She wanted to know just one thing. "How long have you known about this, sir?"

"Only today, Amanda."

She was satisfied with this. It was one thing for Sir Hector to go over her head, but quite another to have been played by a boss who had known all about this and lied to her. "Are you telling me we are finished, sir?"

"Not telling. I'm just wondering whether there's any more to learn."

"What about Preece?" asked Amanda.

Devoy looked at Sir Hector, who shrugged. Clearly Preece was expendable. Sir Hector said, "I'm sure that Mr Preece has done nothing wrong, but you must obviously satisfy yourself on this."

Amanda wasn't really interested in Preece. As far as she was concerned, she blamed Sir Hector and Johns for the whole thing. Gaines and Preece were only a couple of middle managers.

She nodded and, addressing Devoy, said, "I think I agree with you, sir, but there is one major remaining issue. There's a woman in Canish who was part of the original unit. Suzie Miller's her name. She has some knowledge of, and was involved in, some operations." She looked at Devoy very hard. "I would only consider this case closed if I was certain she's no longer in danger. If not, I could not recommend closure."

Sir Hector looked at Devoy for a long moment. "I can't imagine, if the case is closed, that she would be at risk."

Amanda looked at Devoy and he nodded. "In that case, Sir Hector, we don't need to see each other again." She got up and said to Devoy, "Thank you, sir."

Without accepting Sir Hector's extended hand, she left the building and breathed in the filthy, but honest, central London air.

Chapter 47

After the meeting with Sir Hector, Amanda was in no mood for work and instead took a taxi to her Georgian flat in Victoria. She owned it outright, and it was described as a penthouse, which was true to the extent that it was on the top floor of the four-storeyed building. That said, it was far from a humble abode, with a couple of high-ceilinged public rooms and three bedrooms. She could have afforded an even more prestigious address, her divorce settlement had seen to that, but she liked it here.

She changed out of her business suit and slumped down onto the sofa. Her relaxation period lasted about sixty seconds. The phone rang. It was good and bad news. Preece had been found on a small Essex island. Inevitably, he was dead. There was no evidence on his recent movements and not much clarity as to the cause of death.

The voice on the phone kept on talking, but Amanda was already bored. It wasn't always good to be proven correct. Not that she cared for Preece. He had been corrupt and self-serving and miles away from her idea of a public servant. She flicked on the television, which was already reporting the discovery. There were a few kind words, but as Preece had achieved virtually nothing, there was really nothing to say.

The phone asked for instructions. Amanda had caught a little of the details at the end, and she repeated them to confirm her understanding. Full of drugs apparently. She knew this method, often good for celebrity accident/suicide. Picked up, knocked out and pumped full of drugs. That had been the end of Preece and had closed his mouth for ever. She advised the phone to brief the press along the lines of a tragic accident and that was the end of David Preece.

Sir Hector was nothing if not efficient. He was safe, but he was wounded. Amanda had left Emma Dixon with Suzie Miller. Suzie had said she was an efficient administrator, and that was now proven. Detailed notes pertaining to, and a near perfect recollection of, every operation, were now in Amanda's possession. Sir Hector Laing was in the clear for now, but the next interview, if there was one, would be very different.

Amanda switched off the television. She was sick and tired of the case and was sick and tired of her own, hopefully temporary, cynicism. She went to bed and relaxed for the first time in a week.

She slept for a couple of hours, and at about six in the evening she got up, refreshed, poured herself a drink and phoned Jack.

He asked how she had got on and she told him everything.

"It's rotten, but what else could you do?" he said.

That cheered her up. It seemed that his approval was now important to her.

"As far as I can see," Jack went on, "only Brannigan was killed by Lennon, and, well, Lennon . . . that's not certain. I still think it's Val Fraser."

"I spoke to Emma today after her interviews with Suzie Miller. She thinks Val Fraser killed Lennon too. I think you should talk to her about it."

"Okay, I'll catch up with her tonight."

"Fine. Tell her that I'm closed this end and tell her I'm confident that Suzie Miller's safe – that is if nothing else breaks locally."

"And what about Val Fraser?"

"It sounds as though you and Emma are on the same page. Meet her tomorrow and decide a way forward and then give me a ring. I'll be okay with whatever you decide."

Jack said, "And afterwards, hopefully I'll see you in London quite soon?"

"Make it very soon," Amanda said.

Chapter 48

When you both knew that you would never be lovers, it was easier to be friends, and Jack and Detective Inspector Emma Dixon walked arm in arm along the sands of Canish bay on a fine late evening.

He had teased her a bit about her constable, and she happily admitted that they were an item. He didn't mention that he was much younger than her, but she did. Apparently, this had caused some talk in the town. She beamed and was happier than he had ever seen her as she related telling a few folks to mind their own business.

Jack had vaguely wanted to get closer to Emma, but he was mostly genuinely happy for her. Why not? She was free and she was in love, and that was all anyone could ask.

Jack wondered if he would ever be in love again.

Emma interrupted his thoughts. "So, what did Amanda say?"

"Amanda seems to think that we have a similar view on the case."

She smiled. "You first."

He outlined most of what Val Fraser had told him without saying explicitly that she had more or less admitted killing Lennon. Emma considered this information and looked at him hard. "Did she tell you that she killed Bobby Lennon?"

"Not exactly. Did she tell you that?"

Emma looked serious, "No, but I am a detective. I know this area and its people. I can't prove it, but Lennon is far and away most likely to have killed Brannigan, and I think he was stopped before he could kill Suzie."

"Who would want to stop him? No one from out of the area, surely?"

She didn't respond to that. "Val Fraser and Suzie Miller are great friends and," she added with emphasis, "I'm friendly with both of them."

Jack abruptly stopped walking and his heart sank. He could overlook a lot of things, but he was pretty sure this didn't extend to overlooking a police officer nodding through a murder. He needed some moral anchor in this affair, some baseline that that he could believe in and live with.

She was a good detective to the end and read his expression. "No, no. Don't think that. I got to this position yesterday. It's the only reasonable theory still standing. I just can't believe in Suzie killing anyone. I've got no evidence. So, who else is left? I had a word with Val last night. She didn't admit anything, and I can't prove anything. What can I do? The forensic reports have nothing more."

"What about Lennon's gun? Did you search Val's house?"

She looked at him hard, then laughed. "Of course, I did. I'm a detective inspector. We looked everywhere, On the day of Lennon's murder. We found nothing."

"Nothing?"

"Nothing."

Jack cursed inwardly; responsibility for the last judgment was now sitting unwelcomingly on his shoulders. He started walking again. "What do you want to do?"

She considered. "Well, Suzie's safe now, according to Amanda."

"I think we can trust her on this."

Emma nodded. "We will keep the cases open for now. Maybe more evidence will turn up, although that seems unlikely."

Jack reflected that it was certainly unlikely, especially as all the missing guns in the case were in the Irish Sea. He decided Emma didn't need to know this. "London will want the case closed."

"It seems we have a common interest, then." She changed the subject. "What are you going to do with your house when it's finished?"

"I'm not sure. I'm not planning to live here, I couldn't ever leave the north-west, but I'm sure that I'll be down here quite often. I love this area. Maybe I'll get some golf in next time."

She said, "That'll be good. I'll look forward to catching up soon."

He smiled and nodded and said that he wouldn't be a stranger, but really that was just another lie. But after the last week, one more lie could hardly matter.

Loose Ends
by
Adam Parish

Book 3 of the
Jack Edwards and Amanda Barratt mystery series

Also by Adam Parish
The Quartermaster (1)
Parthian Shot (2)

To sign up for offers, updates
and find out more about Adam Parish
visit our website www.adam-parish.com

Printed in Great Britain
by Amazon

80675610R00120